BLACKBURN

BRYNNE ASHER

Text Copyright © 2021 Brynne Asher
All Rights Reserved
No part of this book may be reproduced, scanned, or distributed in any printed or electronic form without permission from the author. Please do not participate in or encourage piracy of copyrighted materials in violation of author's rights. Only purchase authorized editions.
Any resemblance to actual persons, things, locations, or events is accidental.
This book is a work of fiction.

Blackburn
Brynne Asher
BrynneAsherBooks@gmail.com
Keep up with me on Facebook for news and upcoming books
https://www.facebook.com/BrynneAsherAuthor
Join my Facebook reader group to keep up with my latest news
Brynne Asher's Beauties
Edited by edit LLC

OTHER BOOKS BY BRYNNE ASHER

The Carpino Series

Overflow – The Carpino Series, Book 1

Beautiful Life – The Carpino Series, Book 2

Athica Lane – The Carpino Series, Book 3

Until Avery – A Carpino Series Crossover Novella

Killers Series

Vines – A Killers Novel, Book 1

Paths – A Killers Novel, Book 2

Gifts – A Killers Novel, Book 3

Veils – A Killers Novel, Book 4

Scars – A Killers Novel, Book 5

Until the Tequila – A Killers Crossover Novella

The Montgomery Series

Bad Situation – The Montgomery Series, Book 1

Broken Halo – The Montgomery Series, Book 2

Standalones

Blackburn

The Dillon Sisters

Deathly by Brynne Asher

Damaged by Layla Frost

1
YOU'RE WELCOME

Lillian Burkette

"That could've gone better."

Of course, he thinks that. Nothing I do ever seems to make him happy. I, on the other hand, thought the meeting was fruitful and productive. But this man—who also happens to be my boss's boss and the owner of the company—is only ever broody and perpetually sour with me.

I don't spare him a glance.

I've been traveling alone with him for days. I'm tired, sweaty, and I need to get home. But more than anything, I hate that I've allowed all of this to get me down.

Usually, I'm a "the margarita is half-full" kind of gal. I always appreciate a partly-cloudy day because some rays are better than none. If I go out to eat and the meal is divine but the service is lacking, I'll still call it a great night out.

Even the worst of times make me look back and appreciate the best moments in life.

My Gran taught me this. She might be a no-nonsense southern woman, but she also doesn't dwell. "Dwelling will only make your skin sag, darlin'," she'd tell me. "Trust your Gran. Your skin will droop soon enough. No point in dragging it down sooner than necessary."

Gran is the most beautiful person I know and I certainly don't want my skin to wilt sooner than gravity can do its heinous work, so I made the decision a long time ago to be like my Gran.

I choose happy.

I always offer a smile to strangers. Because, really, in a world full of ugliness and divisiveness, there's no universal language more effective than a bit of joy worn on one's face when given freely to another.

But my boss's boss doesn't share my outlook on life—especially toward me. It doesn't matter how many priceless gifts I direct his way, I never get anything more than a frown in return.

Or a furrowed brow.

Or a clenched jaw.

Or narrowed, brooding blue eyes.

And despite his surly disposition, those blue eyes are beautiful. They're framed by long, dark lashes that match his inky hair—hair just long enough that it bends and turns into the sexiest male waves I've ever laid my boring, brown eyes on. I know this because I've studied every curved lock on his head, cataloging it into the file I've labeled *The Boss's Boss* I keep in the back of my brain. I've also memorized the distinct bone structure of his cheeks, the vastness of his shoulders, and his hands.

I love hands. They tell so much about a person and my boss's boss has great ones. They're not the hands of a man who works in an office all day, every day. His are calloused, veined, and he's got a scar running down the top of his thumb that disappears up his left wrist. I want to ask him how he came about that scar, but his sour temperament has never encouraged such a personal question.

"Did you hear me?" Gabriel Blackburn bites. He takes such a tone, I can't ignore him any longer, so I look over as we bump along the rocky, dirt road as we make the long trip back to town.

He's taking up more than his fair share of the backseat with one arm stretched out over the back bench while he leans into his door, his large frame shifted toward me. The breeze blows through his unruly hair since the windows are down as we speed through the rainforests of Nicaragua in the Nissan SUV that's probably over twenty years old. Our driver, Armando, and security guard, Sergio, are in the front and I hear them muttering in Spanish about the "asshole" next to me.

That asshole would be my boss's boss.

Dammit, his wavy-hair game is strong today, thanks to the humidity. He's got a pesky curl that's fallen onto his tense forehead. Just like always, I want to touch it, wind it around my index finger, and give it a good yank since he's always so irritable.

After our long week and knowing what I have in store for me once we get back to the States, I'm struggling to hang on to my positive vibe. It doesn't matter how much I love Central America—the land here is as beautiful as its people—I might as well be holding on to my happy nature with the cheap dental floss ... the kind that always frays and gets stuck between my teeth.

I'm *that* over it.

But instead of losing my temper, I do what I always do—I find my happy. Mustering a lame smile, I do my best to speak over the roar of the engine and wind whipping through the car. "I thought it went very well. They're pleased with our new rollout—I'd even go so far as to say we surpassed their expectations by integrating our internet security products into their new accounting and payroll software. They renewed our services for another year, which is what we came to do. How could it have gone better?"

I've been at my job for only four months, but I've worked in sales in the tech industry for two years. I landed this position, not only because I'm good with clients, but also because I'm fluent in Spanish. Marketing reps are a dime a dozen in the industry, but my bilingual resume—and I'd like to think my winning, upbeat personality—sets me apart. So here I am, peddling our business and internet security software to all of Central America.

The Director of Marketing hired me. I didn't meet Gabe until after I started. My boss was supposed to accompany me on this trip, but he came down with the flu days before we were scheduled to leave. When I found out Gabe stepped up to take his place, I thought I'd die.

Gabriel "Gabe" Blackburn is all business, but since he's the owner and CEO, I guess he doesn't have to worry about winning anyone over. I hear he's a techie at heart—a computer engineer and software programming guru who just happens to live inside the perfect male body.

Really, I shouldn't let him upset me. It's better he has a salty personality. If he were to be charming on top of beautifully rugged, I'm not sure how I'd get through the day or focus on my job.

He catches my eye when he moves, rolling up the sleeves of his linen shirt to expose his tanned forearms that are almost as nice as his hands with that mysterious scar teasing me.

He shakes his head and I know he's glaring at me even though I can't see his blue eyes behind his aviators. Then he bites out, "I had no idea what was going on and you didn't once translate for me."

I raise my brows. "We discussed my plan for the meeting and all we hoped to accomplish. It went smoothly and they didn't have any questions I couldn't answer. I even upsold them on products they hadn't planned to purchase. You never asked me to translate for you and, quite honestly, it would have made the meeting all," I pause to shrug and shake my head, "awkward."

This was our last client to visit this trip. So far, we've been to Mexico, Belize, and Honduras, but those clients were mostly fluent in English. Today, not so much.

Despite his annoyance, I've seen a different side of him with customers on this trip than he's ever shown me in the office. Gabe Blackburn can turn his personality meter up to *charming, with a strong side of sexy intelligence* and the clients melt into a pile of big, gloppy goo in his strong, veined hands. But today, he was forced to sit at my side, not understanding a word. He wouldn't have been able to charm the salt off a margarita glass if he'd had the chance.

He wipes his forehead before running his hand through his hair and flips off his sunglasses. The heat is oppressive. We aren't exactly in business dress, but more Central American business attire. I'm in a Carolina blue wrap dress with chunky sandals. Gabe is wearing a light pair of khakis with a long-sleeved linen dress shirt left open at the neck.

Not done complaining, he continues, "I like to interact with clients. I want them to know I'm involved in the process, not just sitting back at the office not giving a shit what they need. Why do you think I'm here, Lillian? Trust me. This is no vacation."

"I'm sorry," I offer, even though I'm not sorry at all. This is no vacation for me either. I haven't seen the beach once and I've ordered dinner in my room every night to avoid him. Traveling and spending all day with him for an entire week is more than enough. When our days have ended, he's barely offered me a pained "See ya tomorrow" and gone straight to his room.

I could use a fruity drink in a coconut shell right about now—the little umbrella would be the happiest thing I've encountered all week. I can tell Gabe's invested and passionate about the products his company puts out, but I'm not lying. It would have been awkward if all I did was sit there and translate. "I'll do better next time. I'll make it a priority to make sure you're heard."

He scrapes his scarred hand down his face and looks out the window as we bounce along.

"You're welcome," I go on and he looks at me with a scowl. His winning personality has really clawed its way through my *be-happy* mantra over the last six days, causing all my deeply ingrained etiquette lessons to dissolve as fast as my deodorant in this rainforest. I've had it. "You're welcome for the prosperous week. By my figures, I've not only maintained your sales from the last year, but I'm up by sixty-seven percent. You might turn on the charisma for clients, but I'd like to think everything I've done over the last four months to build these relationships has contributed, so you're welcome, again." I shift to face him and lean forward. "You're also welcome for my helping you order lunch the other day when there was no menu. And I said I'd do a better job at translating next time, for which most people would offer a *thank you*, to which I would respond in turn with a very sincere *you're welcome*."

My last word comes out on a huff because the car jumps and jerks. Neither of us is wearing a seatbelt—because there aren't any—and I reach to hang onto the first thing I find, which is his rock-hard thigh. Both our bodies shift and it's only a second before we right ourselves, but when I look up, Gabe's eyes are on me and they're not pissed like I thought they'd be after my tirade. Nor are they apathetic or impatient.

They're fiery—as hot as the afternoon

Nicaraguan sun that's been beating down on us all day. His intense stare drops to my hand that's still wrapped around his thigh—closer to his manhood than his knee, unfortunately—and with a mind of its own, my hand flexes, feeling nothing but muscle.

Oh, shoot. I think I just felt-up my boss. Well, my boss's boss.

I'm like a horny teenager, copping her first feel, rather than a twenty-six-year-old businesswoman.

I release his leg. Not quite sure what to do with my hand at this point, I scoot toward my door, as far away from Gabe as I can get and mutter, "Sorry."

Gabe cocks his head. "Really? Could've sworn you were *welcome*."

Dammit, he's going to fire me for copping a feel *and* for being rude.

"I'm sorry about that, too," I say, genuinely this time and fan myself from the stifling heat and the feel of his thigh closer to his cock than his knee. "Really sorry, actually. I think it's the heat." Who am I kidding? It's him and everything else swirling in my life right now. "Or the long week, I don't know. I'm on edge and lost my words. It won't happen again."

Through all this, Armando and Sergio have begun talking faster and their words catch my attention. Gabe moves his focus from my lame apology to our driver and security guard. "What are they saying?"

Sergio doesn't give me time to translate and looks back to both of us, demanding in his deep accent, "Roll up the windows."

The crank on my side of the car is rusty and stiff.

Gabe rolls his up before I do and growls, "What's going on?"

I look out the front windshield as we slow through the heavy tree cover.

"Go," Sergio demands as he bangs on the dashboard.

Armando doesn't go. Armando continues to slow and starts to argue with Sergio so quickly, I can barely pick up mere phrases because their dialects are strong. I only catch curse words.

My body jolts when Gabe repeats from beside me, "What's going on?"

I look over at him and realize all these months when I thought he was irritated or angry, I was wrong.

This is Gabriel Blackburn angry.

"Go!" Sergio screams and gives Armando a hard shove to get his attention.

"What the fuck," Gabe growls and before I know it, our old Nissan Pathfinder jerks to a complete stop and we're forced to brace ourselves on the seats in front of us. All the air leaves my body when I look through the bug-splattered windshield. Standing in front of us is a group of men. Four scary men dressed in black and green and brown—all carrying very large guns.

Sergio shifts low and reaches for something as he growls in Spanish, "Drive through them!"

"Holy...," I whisper and look over at Gabe.

He doesn't take his eyes off the men standing sentry in front of us, but I know he's talking to me when he murmurs, "Make yourself small and do exactly what I say."

My eyes go big when he surreptitiously reaches for his ankle and, after yanking up his pant leg, produces a gun hidden in an ankle holster.

What the heck?

2

SUMMER CAMP

Lillian Burkette

WHEN I WAS ten, I went to summer camp for the first time. It's not like it was a huge feat or anything. I went with my childhood friends. I'm pretty sure our mothers lived for that first overnight camp when we were gone for an entire week because they booked themselves into summer camp for hoity-toity mothers—the spa.

On the second day of camp, I was on the ropes course. Since I was a puny ten-year-old, it was more than challenging. Sweaty from the afternoon heat, my hands slipped, my feet got tangled. I fell but I never hit the ground. I hung there by one foot, breaking my leg in the process.

Summer camp was over and so was my mother's week at the spa. She was not happy.

During the moments I was waiting for someone

to free me, time stood still. The pain was excruciating and I never thought it would end.

In the back of an old Pathfinder in the middle of a rainforest in Nicaragua, it is not unlike that day at summer camp.

Fear.

I don't think I've ever experienced real fear until this very moment.

And, again, time stands still as I watch our driver, Armando, produce a gun from under his shirt. My scream echoes in my head as he turns and point-blank shoots our bodyguard in the head. Sergio, sitting right in front of me, falls to the side and onto the window, where the back of his head is splattered all over the glass.

My mouth falls open and I jerk when Armando turns that gun to me, but instead of pulling the trigger, he motions toward the door. "Get out of—"

He doesn't get another word out.

He slumps with a thud over the steering wheel and, when I look over, I realize Gabe shot him through the driver's seat. The horn, blasting continually from Armando's dead weight, is polluting the small cab of our old Nissan.

I want to scream and cry and run from the nightmare unfolding in front of me, but I don't get a chance to do any of that. Through the bellows of the horn, I hear shouts from the men blocking our path just moments ago.

I let out another scream when Gabe's hand comes to the top of my head and forces me down in the seat, my head now pressed into his lap. It seems like a lifetime ago I was feeling up my boss by accident.

I hear more gunshots—so many—as Gabe pushes me to the grimy floor of the car. I don't know how there's room for both of us, but he leans over me, giving me a good deal of his bulky weight as more gunfire rings through the forest. Glass shatters and the sound of metal hitting metal pierces my ears, terror shooting through my veins.

Just when I think it will never end, all that remains is the constant horn droning on. My lungs ache—my body begging for oxygen—my brain working hard to catch up. The weight pressing me into the filthy floorboard disappears and, when I peek over my shoulder, Gabe's attention is focused on the massacre that unfolded. His elusive gun is still aimed out the front of the car. Once he sits upright, he leans forward between both seats and grabs Armando from behind, yanking him off the steering wheel. The silence is deafening as I hear dead weight fall to the side.

"You can get up," Gabe says in a low, gruff voice.

Shaking, I push off the floor. Without looking at me, he grabs my arm to help pull me to the seat next to him. All I see is Armando, slumped in a bloody mess, sideways over the center console and poor Sergio, dead, collapsed against the passenger door. Sergio has been with us since we landed in Mexico at the beginning of the week. He was sweet and kind and seemed good at his job. He was vigilant with our security—I have no clue what happened today.

I can't even process, at this moment, why

Armando did what he did. I yelp and jerk when I feel a hand on my chin.

"Shhh." Gabe cups my face and turns me to him. I tense when his other hand comes to my shoulder, sliding down my arm, over my hip, and firmly ends on my bare thigh with a squeeze. He's lost his aviators and his blue eyes are piercing, following his hands down my body before jumping back up to my face. "You okay? Are you hurt?"

Finally finding the oxygen to survive, my chest heaves but I don't answer. I feel my face tense and try to turn back to Sergio, but Gabe's big hand grips me and forces me to look at him where he's shaking his head. "Don't. Focus on me. You're okay. I don't know what just happened, but you're gonna have to be okay because we need to get out of here and by the way the car's smoking, it's gonna have to be on foot."

I swallow over the lump in my throat and do everything I can to fight back my tears.

"Lillian?" he calls for me again, using a tone I've never heard from him before. It's not soft—I doubt Gabe has a soft tone—but it's weirdly reassuring, though it still has a bite to it. "We've gotta get out of here. You with me?"

I don't answer him, but ask, "You have a gun?"

His eyes narrow, but other than that, he doesn't move a muscle.

I ramble on stupidly. "They were going to kill us, weren't they?"

Gabe's brows furrow and he tips his head to study me. At the same time, his hand slides back up to my hip where he gives me a squeeze. "Lillian, stop."

I feel my body start to tremble as the words jumping around my head fly out my mouth. "Oh. They were going to kill us. Maybe not now, but eventually. Armando set us up. This is like ... I don't know what this is like—"

Gabe's thumb brushes my lips to shut me up and yanks me toward him where he presses me into his chest. If there was ever a time when someone needed to get their point across swift and fast, now would be at the top of that list. "Stop. Don't think. We need to get out of this fucking car and off the road before whoever sent these shitheads comes to look for them. That didn't exactly go down quietly. So, stop. Grab what you can carry and let's go."

Held tight to him, his words whip across the side of my face in a minty breath and, if anything has, that gets my attention. His arm is wrapped around my back and he's holding me close as we sit in this smoking car surrounded by death and blood. I have no other choice, so I nod.

"Good." On a squeeze, he gives me one more intense gaze and lets me go. "Grab your bag. When we get to civilization and find a signal, we'll need our laptops, phones, and passports."

He grabs his messenger bag and climbs out the door. I can't help myself. I take one more look at Sergio and my heart clenches.

"Lillian." I look back and Gabe is standing in the open door with his arm outstretched, offering me his hand.

I look at his hand, the one I've looked at so many times, even gushed over it in my head, wishing it belonged to someone nice, someone more pleasant, or just someone who didn't hate me. But it doesn't. It belongs to my boss's boss, who's been walking around with a secret gun on his ankle and who just killed five men, probably saving us from who knows what.

He motions his hand for me to take it again and I can tell he's losing his patience. "If I have to fucking pick you up and carry you, I will, but we need to get outta here. I can't leave you in the middle of the rainforest."

Oh. Yes. We need to get out of here.

Without hesitation, I put my pale hand in his large, tan one. When he wraps his fingers around mine, I grab my tote with my other and let out the breath I've been holding. Gabe pulls me out of the car and, even though it's stifling and hot, I appreciate the fresh air.

That is, until we round the front of the car and I see the results of Gabe protecting us. The four heavily-armed men, dead on the jungle floor.

Gabe throws his messenger bag over his head, hanging it across his body and bends to pick up one of the rifles, along with some extra ammo off one of the dead guys. Slinging all of it over his shoulder, he looks at me in a way he never has before. I feel a little lightheaded and I'm not sure if it's from all the dead bodies or the way his eyes are raking up and down my thankfully alive one.

Giving his head a little shake, he sighs and mutters, "This is going to be interesting. Let's go."

And with that, he turns and disappears into the rainforest. It doesn't matter how much I liked poor

Sergio, I do not want to be left here by myself, so I put one wedged espadrille in front of the other and pray to God I don't see a snake—reptile or the murderous human variety.

I have a feeling summer camp did nothing to prepare me for this.

I had no idea how right I was.

3
HELL

Gabriel Blackburn

HELL.

I'm in fucking *hell*.

And it has not one thing to do with being set up by our driver and ambushed in the middle of a Nicaraguan rainforest. Though, I can't lie, that sucked.

Four months ago, my marketing director came to me with a resume of the perfect applicant, who was not only fluent in Spanish, but who also had industry sales experience. I gave him the green light to hire ASAP. I had high hopes of growing our foreign markets, so finding someone to fill both roles in our time frame was a fucking miracle because the rest of us were struggling to communicate with the clients after our last Spanish-speaking rep left. My hell started when I laid eyes on our new Central America rep. I was shocked.

What wasn't included on her resume was her long, dark blond hair, her fair skin, those deep brown eyes, or lips so perfect I have to force myself to think about my Great Aunt Libby's cats to get my mind off her. Aunt Libby has as many taxidermied cats as she does live ones. And what tops that freak show off is that my uncle stuffs those cats in their basement—DIY style.

What humans aren't willing to admit is that their pets are a representation of themselves. Show me a freak-of-nature pet, ten grand says their humans are weird as shit, too.

Case in point, Aunt Libby is a freak show and so are her cats. It's a weird-ass cat bonanza on steroids that still freaks me out as an adult. And that's saying something. I was a Ranger in the Army and just took out our driver and four armed guerrillas in the jungle, but I still cringe when I think about those damned cats.

Over the last four months, I've had to force myself to focus on those feline freaks—stuffed and otherwise—every time Lillian Burkette's perfect lips curve into a smile so bright, all I can do is wonder what effect those lips would have wrapped around my cock. The way she lights up a room with only her smile, she'd surely send me straight into blowjob utopia, where I'd drift around like a fucking float at the Macy's Thanksgiving Day Parade.

I keep telling myself blowjob utopia doesn't exist, but I'll never be in the position to find out since she's my employee and I don't shit where I live. Also, it would suck—metaphorically speaking—to expect the blowjob of all blowjobs, only to be let down by poor suction, no ball stimulation, or—shoot me with my own gun—if she ignored the tip. It's better to stick to my fantasy than be plagued by bad-blowjob reality.

This is the mantra I've chanted to myself for the last four months right after I think of the dead cats decorating the guest room I was forced to sleep in when I had to visit Great Aunt Libby.

I thought, after time, it would get easier being around Lillian and, in some ways, it has. After four months of ignoring her and wearing her down with the surliest demeanor I could muster, I'm pretty sure she's given up on winning me over. No longer do I get warm smiles, sweet "good mornings," or offers of home-baked delights that smell so damn good when she brings them into the office, I have to make myself not ravish the whole basket in the same way I've dreamed of ravishing her.

It also doesn't help that everyone loves her because she's like the sun, floating around the office, drawing everyone into orbit around her warmth and baskets full of sugary pleasures. She's become everyone's best friend—offering to water plants when people are out of town or babysitting. Hell, she even threw a retirement party for someone in HR last week.

It's not just her personality that's made my associates bring her into the fold like a long-lost child. She's smart and damn good at her job. She wasn't lying earlier. She's grown her territory in huge proportions in her first quarter alone and, from what I've seen all week, clients worship her.

She went from just another beautiful face, to a beautiful face with a rocking body that houses the sweetest and smartest woman any man would fight to have in his bed. Don't even get me started on her voice. So soft, with only a hint of a southern accent that makes everything she says even sweeter.

What's not to love? She's perfect.

Which is why I'm in *utter, fucking hell.*

We left the client at around four o'clock and since the fucking ambush, we've been walking for hours. She's in those sexy sandals that I've tried hard not to look at all day because they do amazing things to her bare legs. Those legs in that dress, in turn, do other things to my cock that I've had to fight off during client meetings. I slowed my pace for her a bit, but even maneuvering in those shoes throughout the rainforest, she's keeping up better than I imagined. Nevertheless, listening to her breathe for hours has been torture.

Damn her for needing so much oxygen.

The sun is starting to disappear and I glance back down at the compass on my phone. We've been moving on a westerly path since we started and haven't come in contact with anything. From my calculations, we would've had at least another hour-and-a-half drive back to town. Which means, we should eventually hit civilization and be able to get back to our hotel. My only concern is who we'll run into when we get there. Two Americans in Central America are bound to draw attention. It's why I hire security and always carry when I'm here, but that wasn't enough this time.

I swipe the large makeshift machete, that's really just a stick, through the brush ahead of me and stop abruptly. Lillian stumbles and grabs onto the back of my shirt to balance herself and my muscles tense at her touch.

"Sorry." She pushes away quickly. "I've been watching the ground so I don't trip."

When I turn to look at her, I put a finger to my lips and shake my head to shut her up. She's close, standing a breath away as she frowns up at me before leaning to the side to peer around my shoulder.

Her face lights up and she whispers, "A house."

I frown and turn to the side, pulling her behind a patch of thick trees and brush. Ever since I laid my hands on her body in the car after the shooting, I've thought of nothing besides touching her again.

Okay. I've also thought about how to get us out of here, dead cats, *and* touching her again.

"Shh," I whisper. "It's nothing but a lean-to and we have no idea if anyone's in it."

"Well, it might not be a house, but it's definitely someone's home. There's a stool out front and some tools—even a pot by the little fire pit. Maybe someone can tell us how to get out of here."

We've barely spoken to one another since we started hiking, so to hear her speak, especially with her words brushing my skin, is fascinating and I have to make myself focus on her deep-brown eyes rather than her lips. She's pulled her hair out of her face and tied it high on her head, with strands that didn't feel like cooperating glued to her fair skin with perspiration.

I do my best to think about the issue at hand and not be jealous of her unruly locks. "Have you forgotten that not everyone out here is our friend? We can't assume someone's just going to welcome us in for dinner."

Her face falls as if I just killed all hope she creatively concocted in her head. But what almost does me in is her fidgeting back and forth on her feet, rubbing her body from her tits to her knees against me. "It's just ... well ... I was hoping we could take a break. I hate to complain, but my feet hurt and I have to go to the bathroom."

"Why didn't you tell me? I would've slowed down even more."

She lifts a shoulder, causing her tit to rub against me. If I don't let go of her soon and get my mind on something else, I'll be forced to steal a cat from Aunt Libby and carry it around with me at all times. It'll be my very own cock-softening, taxidermied pussy. I'll name it Limp Dick. Even it might not do the trick because right now—I'm waging a war against my cock and the more she moves, the harder it is to not become ... well ... harder.

As if she could read my mind, she puts her hands to my chest and pushes, stepping away from me so I'm forced to let her go. "I knew we needed to get to wherever we were going fast and you were on a mission. Plus, moving at a good clip meant there's a better chance I wouldn't see a snake and, at this point in the day, I think a snake might do me in. You seem to know where you're going, right?"

I narrow my eyes. "Generally."

"Oh." She looks to the side and hitches her bag up her shoulder and I notice how dirty she is—we both are, really—from walking through the jungle. Her dress is ripped over her thigh and she's got cuts and scrapes all over her arms and legs from the brush. She slaps a bug on her arm when she goes on. "I guess *generally* is better than being lost, but the sun is going down. Do you have any idea how much farther we'll have to walk?"

I sigh and shake my head, not wanting to admit it out loud. But with no signal, the best I can do is keep us on a straight trek so we're not circling ourselves.

"Okay." Her voice is small and not only does she look worried, but also tired.

"Stay here," I say and her eyes go big. There's nothing around that I can tell—not even an old road leading up to it but I need to make sure it's safe. "I'm going to check out the shack. Maybe we can stay there for the night if it's abandoned. Stay put. You'll be able to see me the whole time."

She nods and I move, making my way to the back of the lean-to. There aren't any windows, but I don't hear anything and, when I get around to the front, it seems deserted. Weeds and brush are growing up through the old fire pit and everything is rusted to the point of falling apart. I step inside carefully and the boards creek under my feet, but nothing seems like it will give way. There are some rags lying around that look like they once might have been blankets along with trash and enough cobwebs to trap Sasquatch.

I step back out and look where Lillian is waiting. "It's all clear. We can settle here for the night."

I watch her move through the last of the brush and walk gingerly to me.

A night with Lillian Burkette.

I had no idea I could fall deeper into hell, but here I am.

4

SUPERCALIFRAGILISTIC

Lillian Burkette

Gabe took off into the jungle like it was his playground and had navigated it a million times. I'm not terrible with directions, but when dropped in the middle of nowhere in a foreign country, I'd have no clue where to go. I was only too happy to follow. Even if my feet had daggers shooting through them from my shoes, I wasn't about to complain or ask to stop.

But, my feet are killing me and I didn't lie—I'm about to pee my pants.

When I walk through the opening of the little house, Gabe is using a branch with leaves on it to clear out the cobwebs and sweep out as much trash and dirt as he can.

Hmm. Gabe Blackburn does housework and, from the looks of it, he's not half-bad at floors.

I make my way across the small room and dig

through my big tote bag until I find my travel packet of tissues. Setting my bag on the floor, I turn to my boss and do my absolute best to keep this professional, which is next to impossible. "I need a moment of privacy. As freaked out as I am about what happened earlier, not to mention my fear of snakes, I would appreciate it if you could stay here and only come out if I scream bloody murder."

Gabe looks up from his makeshift broom and after dragging his eyes over me, raises a brow. "Watch out for poison ivy. That would suck."

I expel all the air in my lungs. Yes, squatting on a patch of poison ivy would suck, but he didn't need to say that out loud. I try to even my voice. "I'll be right back."

I walk around the back of our little shelter and do everything I can to ignore the pain from my shoes. I try to peer into the shack to make sure he can't see me through the aged boards. Thinking I'm safe and not wanting to wander too far, I take care of my business and hurry back. I'm not looking forward to spending time alone with the big boss, let alone all night in an abandoned house with him.

Gabe has made quick work of his chores and is tossing his broom out the door when I return. He gives me a tight look before stepping aside to make room for me.

Going straight to my bag, I dig around and find my hand sanitizer and a bottle of water. After washing my hands, I take a much-needed drink. I did everything I could not to touch it while we were walking, I had a feeling I might need it later.

I offer it to Gabe. "Thirsty? It's all I have but we can share."

He looks from the water to me before taking the bottle without a word. He takes a sip and hands it back. "You should probably conserve that. You never know."

I'm not sure if that's his way of telling me he doesn't think we'll find our way out anytime soon, but I do my best not to think about that. I reach back in my bag and pull out my cucumber and mint facial towelettes and do my best to pretend we're not lost, that we'll find our way out, and eventually get home.

When I think about home, I close my eyes and take a deep breath. We were supposed to fly out first thing in the morning and I'd arranged to fly straight to Wilmington instead of Indianapolis. I spoke to my grandmother's house manager this morning and it's important—now more than ever—that I get home.

I hear a grunt and my eyes snap open as I'm wiping the sweat away from my neck and chest. Gabe is standing across the small shack, leaning against the wall with his arms crossed, glaring at me.

"Do you want one?" I offer.

He sighs and even though we're surrounded by shadows from the setting sun, I can tell his face is tight and his voice is gruff. "I'm good."

I try not to roll my eyes as I throw the used towelette back into my bag before digging to the bottom. When I turn to him, I decide to make the best of things because this could be my chance to finally win him over.

Taking a big breath, I hold out my hands and

offer him a smile. "Peanut M&M's, trail mix, or a granola bar?"

His frown deepens. "What are you, Mary Poppins or something? Is there a lamp in there, too?"

I tip my head and drop my hands, holding the only food I have with me. "You're a *Mary Poppins* fan?"

"Hardly." He drops his arms and stuffs his hands in his pockets. "I have four older sisters and was forced to watch all kinds of shit I didn't want to when I was little."

The thought of big, tough Gabriel Blackburn with the interesting scar on his hand watching classic musicals as a young boy makes me smile, even while lost in a Central American rainforest.

"What?" he bites.

"Nothing." I smile bigger and try again. "I know you have dietary restrictions, but this is all I have. Can you eat any of this? Lunch was a long time ago."

He crosses his arms again and I realize I've never seen him so uneasy. He's probably eight inches taller than I am and built like a brick house. I'm barely five-five and, even in my heels, he dwarfs me. I'm so used to his commanding presence, I find it odd that he looks so uncomfortable in his own skin. "Why would you assume I have dietary restrictions?"

This confuses me. "Because every time I bring treats into the office to share, you've never touched them. Not once. I assumed you had an egg allergy or eat gluten free or you're a vegan or something. Who knows, maybe you eat paleo? Why else wouldn't you want cookies and brownies and cake?"

He shakes his head and sighs. "I'm not vegan and I don't have any food issues."

"Oh." Well, then. I guess that just means he *really* doesn't like me. The stress from the day is beginning to bear down and the need to sit and take my shoes off is overwhelming. I toss the package of M&M's at him and he moves with quick precision to catch it. "Here. I hear a spoonful of sugar helps the medicine go down. Oh, but you already know that, don't you?"

I sit on the dingy, wooden floor and, when I lean back against the wall, I bite back a moan from getting off my feet. When I reach down to unbuckle my sandals from around my ankles and pull them off, I wince.

"Holy shit," he mutters and moves closer to look at my feet.

I knew I was wearing blisters but I didn't think they'd be this bad. These wedges were comfortable in the store, but hiking through the rainforest in them? No way.

Gabe reaches down and tips my ankle to get a closer look. "You should have told me to slow down. I was surprised you kept up as well as you did in these shoes."

"It's fine." I brush him off and yank at the hem of my dress to pull it down my thighs since he's squatting at my feet.

"I'll be right back." Gabe stands and starts for the door.

"Wait. Where are you going?"

"I'll be gone two minutes." He looks back. "Don't you dare come out unless I scream bloody murder."

My face falls. "That's not funny."

"It's also not funny to tease me about watching *Mary Poppins* when I was forced to by my sisters who weren't above using cruel and unusual punishment before I was big enough to kick their asses."

He turns to leave again and I can't help yelling after him, "If you could sing the *Supercalifragilistic* song and click your heels together, I could use a fruity rum drink with a happy umbrella stuck in the top."

I'm not sure, but over the hum of the bugs and other creepy sounds in the rainforest, I swear I hear him laugh.

I didn't think Gabriel Blackburn knew how to laugh.

I didn't think it was even possible for him to smile.

Even so, I hope he hurries the heck up.

5

I'M TOUCHING HER

Gabriel Blackburn

"Ouch."

I'm touching her again.

She moans, but not in a good way.

Not the word or noises a man hopes to conjure in the woman he's been obsessing over for months.

"It stings."

Yeah. Those aren't good words, either.

"It doesn't sting," I argue, just for the sake of something to say. I'm sure it stings like hell.

"How do you know? Did you walk for hours in heels through the rainforest? No, you're a man. You get to wear sensible shoes *all* the time. What are you putting on me anyway?"

"Arrowroot," I mutter as I use my pocket knife to slice off another piece of the plant. It took me all of a minute to find some after I took a piss. "It's native to South America and the Caribbean, and I thought I saw some earlier. It can be applied as an ointment. Aloe would be better but arrowroot can be used in a pinch. It's also a natural cure for colic and can be used as a mild laxative." I look at her and go on. "Should you have a problem with that."

Her eyes widen. "I'm good. I'll stick with the ointment, thank you very much." She winces and tries to pull her delicious leg out of my grasp, but I hold tight to her calf. "How do you know all this?"

I let go and move around to her other foot where she's worn blisters through and some have started bleeding. "I was in the Army."

"Really?"

I'm crouched by her feet, trying to see her sores through the dimming light. We can't afford to use up what battery life we have left in our phones. I don't let her go but look up her bare legs to her curvy figure and find her face, shadowed by the darkness. "Really. Is that so hard to believe?"

She shrugs and her perfect pink lips tip on one side. "Given your love for musicals, it might be a tad bit shocking."

I give her my best glare.

"*Oklahoma*?" she asks.

I frown. "I'm not from Oklahoma."

This time she smiles so big I can see it through the dim light. "No. The musical. Do you like it? Maybe you're a *South Pacific* kind of guy given your service to our country." I ignore her and go back to work on her feet. "*West Side Story*? *The Sound of Music*? *Fiddler on the Roof*?"

"'Even a poor man is entitled to some happiness,'"

I quote before I blow on her little toe that's mangled with an ugly blister and feel goosebumps crawl up her bare leg. I lean back but don't take my hand off her ankle. "My mother taught theatre at my high school. And before you ask, the answer is no. I never got into it, but I did have to sit through every play she ever put on until I left for college."

Her face softens. "Well, that's a side of you I never imagined. Gabe Blackburn—a reluctant bystander of the arts."

"Does it feel any better?" I ask, ignoring her last comment.

"Yes. Thank you."

I move and sit next to her, leaving a good twelve inches between us. Since I'm in hell, I might as well sit close enough where I could touch her even if I know I shouldn't. It's the universe teasing me—tempting me—with the woman I've done everything possible to stay away from. I lean my head back on the wall and pretend I'm not stuck in hell—or Nicaragua—wondering what I did to deserve such torture.

I'm a good business owner. My employees are compensated well above industry average. I give them more vacation time than most and I'm generous when it comes to bonuses. Everyone has choices when it comes to careers and I do everything I can to make my company one of the most sought after to work for. I don't mind offering six weeks of vacation to everyone because when they're at work, they're beasts. My increasing bottom line and market share over the last five years is all the proof I need. I might be a workaholic but it's all I know. I visit my parents regularly. I'm philanthropic. I donate blood. And I do my best not to hit squirrels when they run out in front of my car.

For the life of me, I can't figure out what I've done to deserve this torment.

Of course, she keeps talking, her perfect soft voice making me hungry in a way that has nothing to do with the pains in my stomach. "What did you do in the Army? And I'm not trying to make small talk—it would be great if you could reassure me by telling me you've been trained to find your way out of the middle of nowhere."

I take a breath and feel around on the floor beside me until I find the package of M&M's. Tearing open the top, I shake a few into my hand before holding out the package for her. She still hasn't eaten anything. When she takes the package, brushing my hand with her fingers, I give her my condensed bio. "Went to West Point and majored in IT. When I did my time in the Army, I started as an officer, but applied for Ranger school and got in."

Every minute move she makes hits me like a roar. Her breathing, chewing, the crinkling of the candy wrapper.

She clears her throat. "I guess if I'm going to be lost in Central America, I'm lucky to have you."

Her glowing praise doesn't match her tone—worried and tight with stress. "We'll find our way out, Lillian. I promise."

"Do you always carry a gun?"

"Not always. But when I'm here, yes."

She shifts and when she goes on, I can tell she's turned to face me in the dark. "We flew commercial. How did you get a gun?"

I roll my head toward her voice. "Sergio. I've contracted with him on previous trips and he always provides me a weapon. He knows my background. He was always solid in the past. I'm not sure what happened today."

She fidgets, rustling in the dark, the floorboards creaking under her. Even through the sounds of the forest, I hear her sniff.

"Lillian?"

She sniffs again.

My voice becomes demanding. "Lillian."

"I'm sorry." Her sweet voice is shaky and, fuck me, I think she might be crying. "Sergio was a sweet man. I got to know him over the last week and even though he spoke English, he was chattier in his native language. He had a family—a wife and two small children." She sniffs even louder and lets out a choked sob, apologizing again. "I'm sorry. I think it's all finally sinking in. He showed me pictures of his kids—they're so small. His family lost him and they probably don't even know it yet." Another two sobs escape, tearing through my insides like a jagged knife. I hear her start to move when she mutters, "I need a tissue."

I reach for her and find her bare bicep, wrapping my hand all the way around it. "Wait. Don't get up. You'll get your sores infected."

"I'm so sorry. I'm a mess. I need to blow my nose."

I find myself doing something I know I shouldn't.

Maybe it's being around her so much over the past week, or being stranded together, or sharing this awful fucking experience, but I can't sit here, listen to her cry, and not touch her. "Come here."

She argues as she cries. "No, I'm fine. I'll get myself together—I promise. I just need to blow my nose."

"You can use my shirt." I shift to put my arm around her stiff body, pulling her into my chest for no reason other than I must be a masochist, because if the twelve inches separating us was torture, this will be the end of me. I undo the top three buttons of my shirt to loosen it. "Here, wipe your face. Feel free to blow your nose, it's not like we aren't filthy anyway."

She continues to cry and her voice raises an octave. "I'm not going to blow my nose on your shirt."

I wrap my other arm around her and snake my hand into her hair, lowering my voice. "It wouldn't be the worst thing that's happened today."

This makes her cry harder. Dammit, I'm shit with words.

"I'm sorry," I whisper and press my face into her soft hair. "Sergio was a good man. Today took us all by surprise. I promise to find Sergio's family and do something for them. I don't know what, but something."

Another few sobs escape as she nods against my chest, fisting my shirt to her face.

"Shh," I whisper into her hair. "I promise I'll get you out of here. You'll be okay. Don't think about Sergio right now."

She nods and we don't say anything more about

Sergio or being lost in Central America or musicals. As we sit here listening to the symphony of the jungle, Lillian starts to relax and gives me her weight.

Just when I think she's asleep and I'm forcing myself to think of dead cats instead of the woman in my arms, she whispers, "Gabe?"

"Hmm?" I lean my head back on the wall and close my eyes. She wipes her eyes on my shirt again and I'm pretty sure her nose, too.

"How did you get the scar on your hand?"

I pull in a big breath. "Afghanistan. We got trapped in a shelter and were trying to dig our way out when a grenade was thrown in."

She tenses in my arms and says nothing for many moments.

"Thank you for being sweet," she whispers. "Nothing like this has ever happened to me before."

Hell.

As long as I'm here, I might as well settle in and enjoy it.

I pull her tighter to me. "You're welcome."

6

YOU SNORE

Lillian Burkette

GROWLING.

I blink my eyes open and hear it again. Thank goodness it isn't from some rainforest animal, but rather from a stomach. A stomach that must be behind me because all I see are long male legs stretched in front of me.

I push up on my hands and realize I'm lying on the hard floor, using Gabe's lap as a pillow. Pulling my hand up to rub my neck, I turn around to find him gazing at me, still slouched against the wall.

"Did you sleep?" I ask.

His blue eyes are piercing and I take a moment to appreciate his messy man-waves as he shakes his head. "Not as well as you. You sleep like the dead."

I frown. "I do not."

His eyes widen. "Lillian, it stormed."

My frown deepens. "It did?"

"Yeah. I laid you on the floor, went out to collect as much rainwater as I could in what few containers I could find. Then I patched a small leak in the roof, so I moved you over a few feet so you weren't lying in a puddle of water. Later, I put your head in my lap so you didn't get a neck ache. You don't remember any of that?"

I lick my dry lips, wondering how much water he collected because I'm not only hungry but also parched. Then I promptly lie, "I remember some of it."

I sit here amazed as a smirk appears on Gabe Blackburn's lush lips—the first I've ever seen. It does incredible things to his way-past five-o'clock-shadowed face and reminds me of last night in the dark when he was sweet at a time he absolutely didn't need to be. And how I fell asleep in his arms...

He shakes his head, that smirk deepening as he stands quickly, towering over me. "You're a liar and you snore."

I bring my hand up to my mouth. "No. I snored?"

He squats near my feet and touches me again, inspecting my blisters. "Yeah. You snored. It's quite satisfying to find something about you that isn't perfect. How are your feet?"

I yank at the hem of my dress. "They're okay, but I don't know how fast I'll be able to walk today. I'd cut off my little toe for a pair of flip-flops."

"I promise to go slow. There's no need to go home without all ten of your pink-painted toes. I'll find some more arrowroot and we'll pad the blisters with some of your tissues. Maybe that will help." Gabe stands and holds a hand out for me. He pulls me up and my body complains about sleeping on a wooden floor as I stretch. He hands me a bowl of water. "Here. Drink up."

I take the old bowl. "I assume this has been deemed safe to drink by Army Ranger training standards?"

"I dropped sand in it and it sunk. Without a water testing kit, that's the best I could do."

I look down into the bowl. "Floating sand is bad?"

"Very bad." He lifts his chin for me to drink. "Come on. We need to make use of the daylight. I doubt we'll luck out and find shelter in the forest two nights in a row."

I sigh and put the bowl to my lips. It's not exactly filtered but it's refreshing and I gulp it down, not even worrying about the sand at the bottom.

Yesterday I watched six people get killed—five of them by my boss in order to save us. Today *must* be better, right?

7

REGRETS

Gabriel Blackburn

Fuck. Just when I thought it couldn't get any worse.

As she slept through the storm last night, I talked myself into the fact it doesn't matter that she's my employee. That I could step over the line, take a risk, and do what I haven't allowed myself to.

I could take her and make her mine.

That is, if I can win her over after acting like a class-A asshole all this time.

All morning, we've hiked as slow as she needed with me bulldozing the way through the brush for her. I've asked her about her life, her family, her education, and what drove her to become multilingual.

I've learned that she's an only child, she's from the south—which explains her sweetness, and she had a crush on her seventh grade Spanish teacher. She laughed at me when I frowned at the mention of her childhood crush and she told me not to worry. There wasn't a scandal because the middle school star point guard, Cody Worthington, swept her off her schoolgirl feet and was her first kiss.

It was then I decided I fucking hated Cody Worthington and, should he ever cross my path, I might send him an email that would fry his hard drive faster than he put the moves on my sweet Lillian back in the day.

Then she told me she missed her flight this morning to North Carolina. Her voice wobbled with worry when she said her grandmother wasn't doing well—as in really not well—and she was supposed to see her this weekend.

I stopped in my tracks and she almost ran in to me when I asked why she was in Central America if she had a family emergency.

The look on her face said it all and it cut deep. She didn't need to back up her awkward expression with words, spelling it out that she was here because her boss's boss is an unapproachable fuckwad.

That was the moment I focused on nothing but her, deciding I'd do everything I could to get her to her family—fast.

That was also the moment I lost focus.

I never lose my focus.

But seeing her tied and gagged after being manhandled and thrown into the bed of a truck, I've never regretted anything more.

8

THIS ISN'T GOOD

Lillian Burkette

JUST WHEN I thought nothing could be worse than yesterday, they came out of nowhere. They might as well have clawed their way out of the ground. One moment, we were standing in awkward silence as I tried to come up with an excuse why I didn't have the courage to cancel my work trip, and the next, we were surrounded.

It was four-on-two and I'll never forget the look in Gabe's deep blue eyes. Given I've been no help since this whole nightmare started, it might as well have been four-on-one. Gabe did all he could and grabbed me, pulling me into his chest, but this time we didn't have the cover of a vehicle to protect us. They yanked me out of his arms, took his weapons, and then threw me to the ground. I couldn't see what they did to Gabe, but I heard.

Screaming and writhing—I did all I could but it was no match for my opponent. He had me bound and gagged—effectively shutting me up—in quick order. When I was flipped to my back, I saw.

Gabe was on his side, moaning from what looked like a hit to the head. The guns he was carrying had been tossed to the side and they had him tied, just like me.

Sitting across from me, Gabe was also gagged. But from the moment we were tossed into this truck, he hasn't taken his eyes off me. As we bounce along this makeshift road surrounded by armed thugs, I cringe at what I hear.

It was their friends Gabe killed yesterday and they know he owns a company. They're expecting him to pay up big for our release. I have no idea what his bottom line looks like, but they're angry about losing their comrades and have upped the ante because of it. They chat freely, not knowing I understand what they're saying. But when they start talking about me—their plans for me and how much they'll enjoy it—I know it shows on my face.

Gabe's eyes bore into mine and he gives his head one little shake.

He doesn't understand what they're saying, but maybe it's their laughing or the way they're leering at me, he seems to know. Squeezing my eyes shut to keep my tears at bay, I know I can't let on that I know what they're saying.

I need to focus and not freak out. Maybe this will be my way to help.

I swallow hard and open my eyes to look to my

boss. A man who, before yesterday, I swore hated me. But since our nightmare started, he's been different. The beautiful asshole with the bluest eyes I've ever seen, sexy hair, and the most amazing hands on earth, has been a different man.

He's been sweet, caring, and, because of it, when he lays his hands on me, I melt in a way that has nothing to do with the humidity.

So, I listen but focus on Gabriel Blackburn. My boss's boss, the person who I pray can get us out of this mess, and the man I'm seeing in a whole new light.

―――

ONCE WE GET to their camp—which was like the Biltmore Estate compared to where we slept last night—they throw us into a back room where they're taking turns guarding us. They have electricity and radios. I even saw computers when we walked in, albeit, they weren't state-of-the-art. I can only imagine what Gabe, being the master of all things tech, thought of their set-up.

We haven't had anything to eat or drink since this morning and the sun has all but set. Gabe and I are on opposite sides of the room facing one another. We're both tethered to hooks attached to the floor—our wrists bound behind us. Their medieval contraptions don't make me feel any better about our situation. Metal hooks screwed into the floorboards scream they're in the business of kidnapping and probably have it down to an artform.

And here I thought I'd be sitting with my Gran at this very moment, if she hasn't taken another turn by now. She's been the only positive constant in my life.

It kills me I'm not with her. Things really aren't looking good at this point.

Other than the fact they've removed our gags. It's the only thing I have to be thankful for at the moment, so I'm focusing on the pleasure of not having a dirty rag stuffed in my mouth.

Even though Gabe and I can speak, we haven't. He hasn't initiated it and I take that to mean I shouldn't either. Instead, I focus on his intense gaze that lingers from me to the guard and back to me again. I'm doing my best to decipher his blue-eyed, telepathic messages while focusing on what our captors are talking about.

None of it is good for Gabe or me.

They've sent messages—to whom, I have no idea—and now they're waiting.

We're all waiting.

They've also talked about separating us which scares me more than anything so far. If they try to take me away from Gabe, I don't know what I'll do.

And I'm hungry—I'd literally kill someone for a brownie right about now. There are plenty of people around me I would willingly use as targets, that's for sure.

Gabe's face tenses as an engine starts up outside. His eyes dart to the guard whose eyes have been on me way more than I'm comfortable with. We hear one of the cars that was parked out front drive off.

Luckily there isn't anyone else here—the four thugs who took us hostage are enough.

Shouts in Spanish come from somewhere else in the worn building. I recognize the voice of the man who's been barking orders since we got here, while the others somewhat grudgingly carry them out. He informs our guard that the other two have gone home for the night and he still hasn't heard back from anyone at Gabe's company.

My eyes flit to Gabe, but I barely have time to register his still hard eyes and blank expression when I hear the next order barked through the darkened space.

I've done all I can to stay calm, to pretend I don't know what they're saying, and make myself focus on the man whose arms I liked sleeping in last night more than I should have. The only way this whole situation has been tolerable without my freaking out in epic proportions has been seeing my boss in a new light. I've let my imagination go to places it shouldn't while being held hostage in Central America.

My thoughts have traveled long and far. Gabe owns the company I work for and there's an imaginary, but very important, line that can't be crossed. I'm crazy to go there.

Maybe it's self-preservation, a mental vacation getaway from the situation I'm sitting in. Or, maybe, it's just plain perversion. After he tended to all the sores and blisters on my feet, I couldn't help but imagine those strong hands on me in other ways— better ways. That mouth that blew the sting away on my little toe, relieving other aches in a way I'd beg him for.

But I can't escape and I can't stay calm any longer. My heart races and my blood turns cold despite the sticky, warm night air. The thing I fear most is about to happen—they're going to separate us.

"No!" I scream without thinking and push myself back against the wall, willing myself to disappear.

When I look at Gabe, he's tenser than ever and glaring at the guard—focused on his every move.

The guard props his rifle in the corner before stalking my way and moves in front of me, blocking my view of Gabe. Sneering at me, he mumbles something about how he lucked out to be on duty tonight and when he bends to unlock my handcuffs, I do everything I can to fight him off.

I kick. I scream. I writhe.

I hear nothing besides my cries and the snickers from the man who's wrestling me as he unlocks my cuffs. He's bent over, trying to hold me as I do everything I can, which is practically nothing compared to his painful hold on my forearm pulled up my back. The more I jerk and pull, the more pain jolts through my body from his vice-like grip.

Just when he gets my second cuff released, I pull my arm around to try and claw at him. He moves to stand but I refuse to cooperate, forcing him to pull my weight. When he starts to yank me toward him, I'm suddenly dropped—falling to the floor, but not with nearly the same thud as the big body behind me.

I turn to find our guard laid out, blood seeping

from his head where he hit the wall when he went down hard. Looking over the limp body, I see Gabe is stretched out as far as possible and I'm pretty sure he just kicked the legs out from underneath the guard.

"Get his gun and unlock me, Lillian," he whispers. "Hurry."

With quivering hands, I grab the keys and stand, stepping over the guard.

Gabe turns his head—his face is so close to mine I can feel his breath on my skin as he encourages me with his steady words. "You've got it. One more and we're good."

Heavy footsteps fall upon us at the same time the last *click* turns on his handcuff. He pulls me behind him and before I know it, he's up, off the floor, and, as soon as the big body clears the doorway, Gabe charges.

As if it's his life mission to take down this man, Gabe goes at him. I would never have guessed the owner of a tech company could move the way he does, especially since his last meals were only made up of peanut M&M's and half of a granola bar.

His actions are swift and effective and, now that it's one-on-one, my boss is getting back for what they did to him earlier. And he's doing it in spades.

The guy finally has a free moment to go for his gun, but Gabe goes at him from underneath, catching the bottom of his jaw, causing his head to snap back as he stumbles. Gabe grabs the gun and turns it on our lead captor. He takes no time to ponder. He pulls the trigger as if the choice was as easy as chocolate or vanilla—and everyone knows, it's always chocolate.

The second the captor hits the floor with a bullet through the head, the guy in front of me comes to and rolls. When he climbs to his feet, I yell, "Gabe!"

Gabe turns and just as easily as he did before, he lifts his arm and shoots. I jump as the guy falls to the floor right in front of me.

I stare at the seventh and eighth dead bodies I've now seen in the matter of about thirty-six hours, my chest heaving, and I can't seem to move.

"Lillian."

I look up and Gabe is sliding the gun into the back of his pants as he moves forward to hold a hand out for me. I want to move—I know I need to move—I just don't know if I can.

But I make myself because I don't want any space between us. Someone will have to kill me before I leave his side.

He pulls me up, but he doesn't stop there. He takes a step and presses me into the wall, his big, muscular body covering every inch of mine as he takes my face in his big hands and, before I know it, his mouth crashes on mine.

Gabriel Blackburn, my boss's boss, the asshole who hasn't been an asshole since our lives turned upside-down, is kissing me.

I feel all his pent-up energy released in our connection. His lips are warm and firm as they consume me. His body is solid and I lift up on my toes to get all of him. When he presses his tongue in my mouth, I take it eagerly.

How did him hating me turn into this?

I have no idea and right now, I don't care.

His greedy hands move down my body, squeezing and touching every curve—the sides of my breasts, my waist, my hips—landing like vices on my bottom as he pulls me into him. His cock, long and hard between us, is pressed into my stomach. I almost forget where we are and what's happened to us.

He pulls his lips away from mine with a groan I feel rumble against my breasts. Gabe tips his forehead down and rests it on mine as he breathes hard. "Lillian. No one's going to touch you but me. Do you understand? We need to get out of here but, trust me, we'll get back to this later."

I nod because no one but him touching me is something I could get used to.

He leans down, his eyes level with me and his voice is low, yet rough. "What did he say? You've been calm all day until there at the end."

I shake my head, not wanting to say it out loud.

His blue eyes narrow as he repeats himself forcefully. "What did he say, Lillian? Tell me—now."

My voice is shaky and I have to swallow to get the words out. "He was going to take me away from you, but not far enough where you couldn't hear…"

My words trail off because the expression on Gabe's face turns to stone and his blue eyes to ice when he mutters, "I wish I could kill them all over again. I'd make them suffer long and slow—they'd beg me to put them out of their misery."

I don't agree with him because him killing them quick was just fine with me.

"Nothing's going to happen to you, do you understand?" he goes on and I nod as he rests his forehead on mine. "I'll get you home to your grandmother."

I try to manage a small smile as I lick my dry lips, causing his eyes to drop to my mouth.

When he looks back up again, he gives his head a small shake. "We need to find our way back to civilization. We need to eat, shower, and find somewhere safe to stay so I can get my mouth on you again where we're not surrounded by dead bodies."

Wow. I never imagined anyone could make my panties wet while talking about dead bodies, but Gabriel Blackburn sure did it.

9

TECHNOLOGY

Gabriel Blackburn

I couldn't help myself. I had to kiss her. Touch her again. Let her know how I feel. Throw all fucks aside and do what I've fought against for months—lay claim to her.

I don't give a shit about the rules anymore. There's nothing like life and death experiences to make me realize it's time to obliterate the line and take what I want. From here on out, that's exactly what I intend to do.

Because I want her.

And I didn't lie. I'll never let anyone hurt her again.

I have to taste her one more time, so I lean in where I still have her pinned against the wall in this godforsaken shithole and put my lips on hers. The look on her face is something I'll never forget and it has nothing to do with what we've just been through.

"Let's get out of here," I say.

She licks those damn lips and, if we were anywhere else, I'd yank her dress up and take her here and now.

What comes out of those beautiful lips surprises me. "Yes. I could use some chocolate."

Standing amid dead bodies in a room where we've spent most the day shackled, I can't believe it—I almost smile.

But I wasn't kidding. We need to get out of here.

I drop my hands but grab one of hers to keep her close as we step over lifeless bodies. I peek out the door and see there's a light on at the end of the hall of this ramshackle of a building.

"I'm pretty sure they were the only ones left from the way they talked. The other two went home for the night," Lillian says, speaking quietly.

Without looking back, I mutter, "What else was said today?"

"They're waiting on a reply from your company about the ransom. I'm not sure if you should be concerned or not, but no one responded." I look back at her and her eyes are big. "I mean, don't you think they would have at least responded?"

I shake my head. "They better not have. If these assholes think they're gonna get a dime out of me, they're mistaken. But them contacting corporate is a good thing. That means the authorities are involved and, by now, I hope, the Embassy."

The building is quiet and since she said there was no one else here, I move down the hall toward the light.

"Please don't tell me there's a company protocol for when employees are taken hostage in foreign countries. I might have to start looking for a new job," she says.

I'm forced to look back and frown. "You're not looking for a new job, Lillian."

Her eyes go big. "If this is how many of your business trips end up, I might."

I shake my head and we turn the corner into a room filled with gold. Not literal gold, but given our situation at the moment, we've hit the jackpot.

Technology—it's a sight for my sore eyes.

A computer—even though it may be ancient, might connect to something. Two-way radios and some other ancient shit I'm sure won't help us. A few cell phones laying around. But, a landline.

Who has landlines anymore?

I only need to make one international call and he'd better fucking answer.

The sun has completely set, but I notice another truck parked outside. Now, I just need to find the keys —I haven't hotwired a car in years.

I let go of her hand to pick up the cordless phone and dial, grateful I have a knack at memorizing numbers. Turning to the woman who's made me cross every boundary, I watch her hug herself across her now dingy dress that makes her no less beautiful.

"Do me a favor and start looking for stuff. Car keys, money, food, water ... a new pair of shoes for you. Anything we might need." I start banging through drawers and Lillian starts to do the same.

"Who are you calling?"

I'm about to answer her when he finally picks up and bites, "Who's this?"

I knew he'd answer. Only those close to him have this number and I know for a fact he's gotten many *unknown callers* before.

"Vega," I breathe his name in relief through the dirty handset. "Blackburn, here. I'm in a bit of a situation."

"Fuck, Gabe. What happened? Never mind. Now that I've got you on the phone, I can get you traced. A bit of a situation, my ass. Your VP reached out when they got the first ransom call. I've tried locating you, but you have no signal. Your employee still with you?"

I reach up and brush Lillian's cheek, tucking a piece of hair behind her ear and watch her eyes warm. "Yeah. She's with me. We've had quite the ride but she's still in one piece."

I hear him typing away in the background. I met Crew Vega through a buddy I met when I was in the service. Vega is highly connected and I don't know the half of what he does. All I know is he runs an operation out of Virginia that extends throughout the globe. Vega is solid and I trust him with my life. And right now, I need him to find me and get us to fucking civilization.

"There you are." He keeps pecking away on his keyboard. "Man. You're smack in the middle of Nicaragua. You need to reevaluate your clientele."

"Crew, I just took down two armed guards and I don't know when the other two will be back. I don't want to go back to the hotel—we'll have to leave our stuff. They took our phones, computers, and passports. No idea where they are and I have no money on me."

"Aha!" I hear Lillian from behind me. I turn and she's looking down into a pouch and flipping through a large stack of American dollars with some Nicaraguan córdobas mixed in. She looks up to me and her face lights up. "Lunch money, should we run into a food truck on our way back to town."

Despite our current conditions, I smirk as Vega keeps talking. "You on foot?"

"Hope not." I look back out at the truck, willing it to have gas. "There's a truck outside. We came from the capital, but I'm not going back to that hotel. We need somewhere safe to go then get to the Embassy since we don't have passports and I don't see our shit anywhere around here."

"Found you on satellite maps. There're dirt roads that should get you back to Managua. Keep a southwesterly route. The first major city you'll hit will be Teustepe. You'll find signs toward the capital from there. I'd say you've got a good three-to-four-hour drive, minimum. Call me as soon as you hit civilization. I'll find a safe place to settle for the night."

When I open another cabinet, I find more weapons and ammo. I grab all four handguns and extra magazines. If we can get out of this country without using another gun, that would be better than okay, but I'm gonna do everything I can to cripple their organization before we leave.

"Do me a favor and call Smith. Tell him we lost our passports—he's got government connections.

He'll know who to call. Also, have him look into transportation. We need to get to..." I hold the phone away from my mouth and turn to Lillian. "Where does your family live in North Carolina?"

She's unearthed some gum and is popping a piece in her mouth. She gives me a small frown and says, "Wilmington."

"Tell Smith, when we get out of here, we're going straight to Wilmington, North Carolina. He needs to make that happen. We found some cash, but a credit card would be nice."

"I'll let him know. Call me back if you can't get that truck started."

"We'll talk about that when I step foot on American soil. I'll check in when I can find a phone."

"Talk to you then."

I hang up and turn to Lillian.

"All I found was the cash, gum, and some really, really questionable-smelling bowls of mostly eaten ... something or other. I think it's been sitting around for a while. I'm sorry, but I'd rather be hungry than sick. I don't think I can eat it."

I nod. "I'm gonna go check their pockets for keys and then we'll get out of here even if we have to walk."

She cringes the second the word *walk* passes my lips.

"Stay here," I say.

"Oh, don't worry. I'm not going anywhere without you."

Careful of the blood seeping all over the floor, I check all their pockets and we luck out.

Keys.

I jingle them on my way back down the hall and Lillian's eyes get big when she sees them.

"As long as it's gassed up, we're good to go. Let's get the hell out of here."

She gives me a genuine smile and it lights up my world on this dark night.

10

STARVED MAN

Gabriel Blackburn

WE MADE IT to Teustepe.

It took all of the four hours Crew said it would and then some because of the treacherous makeshift roads. I did everything I could to divert Lillian's mind from what we've been through and what could've happened or could still.

I felt like a starved man desperate for time with her, like I was chained in an enforced captivity by not allowing myself any contact. I was greedy for anything Lillian Burkette.

She answered more questions for over two hours as we drove through the dark rainforest before she started yawning. I told her to lay down on the bench and take a nap.

With hesitant eyes, she finally relented. I guided her head to my thigh and pulled the tie out of her hair as I white-knuckled the steering wheel, trying to control myself as I touched her. Her hand came up and gripped my thigh as I pulled my fingers through her hair until she finally relaxed.

I can pretty much say with full certainty—the woman can sleep anywhere and through anything. Never seen anything like it. She even snored again.

Now, with Lillian still sleeping in the truck, I'm standing on the side of the road at an old payphone.

"Will you accept a collect call from Gabriel Blackburn?" the operator asks when Crew answers.

I hear my friend chuckle and he has the nerve to say, "I guess so."

"Damn, Vega," I start when the call goes through. "I'll pay you back for the call."

He laughs. "Been a long time since I've gotten a collect call, man. Didn't even know it was still a thing."

I get down to business because I feel like a sitting duck. "What do you have for me?"

"I've got a place secured in Managua where you can stay tonight. It's owned by an American. He's a retired Marine and has a place he stays there while on business. It's only a one-bedroom condo—it's the best I could do on short notice."

I look back at the truck where my employee that I've crossed the line with is sleeping. We haven't been separated for days and I'm not excited for that to happen now. "Don't worry about it. We'll make do."

"Smith is working with the Embassy. Your temporary paperwork to get back into the US should be ready late afternoon. I don't know how he pulled that off."

"Smith was CIA. You could get to know him if you came and worked for me."

I hear him smile. "Nice try. I already have an in with CIA."

"How about getting home?" I ask.

"Smith and I are both worried about your name circling—no way do we want you at the airport in the capitol. He contracted a private jet. It'll be there to pick you up tomorrow. He couldn't get it arranged sooner. But that'll give you time to get your paperwork from the Embassy. You'll be flying out of a small airstrip and Smith assured me no questions will be asked when you leave."

I exhale, grateful for the friends I've made and kept over the years. "Perfect."

"You armed?" he asks.

"Yeah. I grabbed a Glock and a couple other handguns. I think I have enough cash to gas up and get us to Managua. Give me the address."

I memorize the directions and how to get into the condo.

"You're a lifesaver, Vega."

I hang up and head back to Lillian. We need food, new clothes, and a shower. It seems like we'll be hiding out in the capital for a day before we can get out. I'm going to do everything I can to find Lillian chocolate and a rum drink in a coconut shell with an umbrella that will hopefully make her smile.

11

THIS

Lillian Burkette

"L ILLIAN, BABY. WAKE up."

A warm, strong hand is on my bottom and I have to admit, here in Nicaragua where we've had to fight for our lives and crossed every professional line that would embarrass my mother to no end—I like it there.

My eyes fly open and, for the second day in a row, all I see are Gabe's legs. I squeeze his muscled thigh and when I arch my back to stretch, he gives me a squeeze through my dress.

I turn my head to look up at him and barely find the morning light peeking through the bug covered truck windows like glitter. My voice is scratchy when I offer him a small smile. "Good morning."

His hand comes up, stroking my cheek with his calloused fingers and shakes his head. "I couldn't hear the radio over your snoring."

My eyes go big. "Stop it. I do *not* snore."

He smirks.

I frown.

His smirk grows into a satisfied cocky smile and he raises a brow, silently relaying to me how loud I snore.

I push up from his lap but before I can get to a sitting position, he turns me and I'm wrapped up in his arms. One of his hands sneaks up into my hair and he takes my mouth.

Grabbing onto his shoulders to hang on, he somehow twists me into his lap as he devours me in his kiss. We're all tongues and hands—my soft to his desperate. When he finally lets go and presses his forehead to mine, we're both breathing hard and, somewhere in the back of my brain, I'm thankful for the minty gum I found in that hellhole last night. We haven't brushed our teeth in days.

"If listening to you snore means I get to sleep next to you, baby, my ears are open and willing for as long as you'll have me."

I close my eyes, embarrassed and turned-on. How is that even possible?

"I said this yesterday—never seen anything like it. You could sleep through a hurricane."

I open my eyes and shrug. "I'm a sound sleeper, what can I say?" I look around and see we're back in civilization. Forgetting all about my snoring, I shift in his lap to take in our surroundings. "We're back? Gabe, you got us back!"

He groans when I move and pulls me down tight into his lap. "We don't fly out 'til tomorrow but I've got a place for us to stay tonight. Let's go get some clothes and food. I'm ready to be settled and safe while we're waiting for our paperwork from the Embassy."

I turn back to him, bringing my hands up to his scruffy, dirty, beautiful face that's now bruised on his temple. For the first time since this started between my boss's boss and me, I press my lips to his. "Thank you, Gabe."

"And we need to find out how your grandmother is. You can make that call when we get settled."

I nod, trying not to tear up thinking about Gran.

He runs his hand down my thigh and gives the torn hem of my dress a tug. "As much as I've liked you in this the last few days, I think we need some new clothes. Let me take you shopping."

I do everything I can not to think of this man as my boss and melt in his arms. "Who are you, Gabriel Blackburn? Until we got lost in the rainforest, you did nothing but scowl at me and now you want to take me shopping? Those five little words are like a dream come true to some women."

His blue eyes gaze intensely into mine. "Let's get moving so I can make sure you're safe until we can leave. We need to talk about *this*," he gives me a squeeze, "before we get back on American soil."

This.

I roll my lips in and take a big breath. This wasn't supposed to happen. *This* should never happen. It's all kinds of unprofessional. Whatever this is, it will have to end when we get back and that makes my insides ache.

But right now, Gabe is going to take me shopping for clean clothes. I might just demand some flip-flops and a toothbrush.

12

NOT GOOD NEWS

Lillian Burkette

I FEEL ALMOST like a new person. It's amazing what a shower, clean clothes, and a toothbrush can do for one's demeanor.

Shopping in Nicaragua isn't like just swinging by the mall. There's no Victoria's Secret or Nordstrom as a one-stop shop.

No. Gabe whisked me through an open-air market and I was in heaven. I've always loved shopping in the markets every time I've been here. I ended up with a maxi dress with spaghetti straps and a pair of wide, loose-fit pants with a matching cami. Gabe bought two pairs of shorts, a t-shirt, and a soft, short sleeved blue button down that will do amazing things for his eyes.

What they do not have in the open-air markets in Nicaragua are panties. Or bras, for that matter.

After schlepping through the rainforest for days

and being man-handled by guerrilla terrorists, there was no way I was putting on that dirty bra and pair of panties. I'll happily go without.

Then we bought local fruits, meats, cheeses, and some veggies off the street. I could have died when Gabe threw in some dark chocolate and a bottle of rum.

When I raised a brow at the rum, he said he didn't have any happy umbrellas, but he could make me a fruity rum drink and said I'd earned it.

I didn't argue.

Then he threw in a bottle of whiskey for himself and we were off again, Gabe informing me that once we got to the condo we weren't leaving until we were on our way to the airstrip. I wondered if that meant we were going to talk about whatever this is that's happening between us.

We took turns showering, ate, and Gabe sat down next to me and asked who I needed to call to check on my grandmother. Unfortunately, that meant calling my mother. He asked for the number and after punching in a slew of numbers, he handed me the house phone in the condo. Then he pressed his lips to my forehead before heading out to the balcony to give me some privacy.

It was not good news.

That was an hour ago.

I shiver. I don't know if it's the AC after being stuck in the heat for days or if it's the news about my grandmother, but I have a chill I just can't shake.

I'm sitting sideways on the sofa, watching the sun slink away for the day. Gabe settles in behind me, wrapping an arm around my waist and pulling me into his chest. He smells clean and all man from the whiskey neat he's been sipping. Ever since I got the news about my grandmother, Gabe has been attentive and sweet—nothing like the man I've known for the last four months. I'm working on a stiff rum drink he made me. I don't even ask what's in it, I just know it's delicious.

He hands me a fresh glass as he wraps me up in his arms. "You're covered in goosebumps. Why didn't you tell me you were cold?"

Not thinking about him being my boss is selfish but I don't care about right or wrong. I allow myself to sink into his warm chest and ask, "Whose condo is this?"

He takes a sip of his drink and sets it on the table, running his hands over my bare arms to warm me. "I don't know."

I turn to look at him. "You broke in?"

He frowns at me. "No. I only break into things when it's absolutely necessary. My buddy arranged this. It's owned by a friend of his, so it's safe. We don't have to worry about anyone being paid off for details on an American businessman and his beautiful female associate."

I sigh. "I've always loved it here. Do you think you'll ever figure out who targeted us? I've been here so many times and never had any problems."

"I doubt we'll ever really know what happened. I need to take a closer eye on security for future trips. I'll bring you back someday and not just for work."

I tense in his arms. "Gabe, we need to talk about—"

He shakes his head, his scruffy beard pulls through my hair. "No. We're not talking tonight after you got the news about your grandmother. You relax and let me get you to Wilmington tomorrow. That's all that matters."

I feel a lump form in my throat and my eyes burn with moisture. I shake my head and bite my lip so hard I taste copper, but I can't overcome it. I've fought it off ever since I got off the phone with my mother. She might have given me the news, but she sure as hell did it with the edge of her tongue for me not being there, telling me all about the time she's had to invest pretending she even cares what happens to her own mother, and finally, for me allowing my *unnecessary and demeaning job* to get in the way of family affairs. All I heard about was how she had to explain to all their friends and acquaintances why I wasn't there.

Appearances. Money. Status.

It's all my mother ever cared about and, when her own mother is on her deathbed, she hasn't changed a bit.

After she rattled off the word *hospice*, I needed no more information. I knew.

"Lillian, I'll get you to your family. I promise." Gabe's strong and steady voice is so close, so warm. I think it's his comforting me that makes my tears break through their barrier. When he realizes I'm crying, he takes my drink out of my hand. "Fuck. Come here."

He turns me to him, sliding a thick arm under my legs and the other up my back. I wrap my arms around him, burying my face in his neck, and the next thing I know, for the first time in days, I'm settled in a soft bed, but this time, with Gabriel Blackburn wrapped around me.

Gabe pulls me tight to his body and strokes my hair and face while shushing my cries.

"I'm s-s-sorry," I try. "But hospice is there—it's bad. I just don't know what my life will be like without her. She's the only g-good part about my family. I'm going to miss her so much."

"Dammit, Lillian. I'm so sorry you're not there. Sorry you felt like you had to be here this week because of me. It's my fault."

I shake my head against his chest, not wanting him to blame himself. "It just happened. It's no one's fault."

"We'll leave first thing in the morning. We have our passport papers all set. Try to sleep."

I feel a little bad about wiping my face on his new t-shirt, but he's holding me so tight and I don't want to get up for a tissue.

He traps my chin in his fingers and lifts my face to his. This time he kisses me soft and slow, easing the pain in my heart with each swipe of his tongue. When he stops, he closes his eyes and breathes against my lips in a way he's holding back, keeping some secret that's causing him pain.

"You didn't sleep at all last night. I should go to the sofa to sleep, since I snore and all," I say.

His eyes open and then narrow on me just as

quickly. "If you even think about leaving my arms, Lillian, we're gonna have issues."

With that, he grabs a blanket and pulls it over us before wrapping me back up. Since I don't want to have issues with my boss's boss, I decide to stay right where I am. He's the one who has to listen to me snore and I offered him a reprieve.

I try not to think about my sweet Gran, Gabe being off limits, and especially my exhausting mother. I settle into Gabe and with the sun barely hanging on to its last rays of the day, we both fall asleep.

Either Gabe is lying about my snoring or it's only taken him two days to get used to it, because we didn't move away from one another's touch all night.

13

FOREVER IS A SAPPY FUCKING WORD

Gabriel Blackburn

When I was serving as a Ranger, there was nothing like the feeling of finishing a mission with all my brothers safe and accounted for. Never thought anything would top that high of being on my way home with all the shit of an assignment behind me.

Until today.

Speeding down the runway with Lillian safe at my side, I hadn't realized how tightly I was wound.

I was exhausted last night but stayed awake until Lillian fell asleep. I called Crew one more time to check in and make sure plans hadn't changed. He assured me the plane would be fueled and ready to go, then asked why we were headed to North Carolina instead of Indy. When I explained, he asked if he needed to book the private jet back to Indy after I dropped off my marketing rep. Crew was surprised to hear I planned to stay in Wilmington.

I'm thirty-five. I never had time for a woman when I was in the Army and, since I got out, I've spent all my time building my business. I've been with women here and there, but no one ever kept my interest and I've certainly never been obsessed with a woman before.

Ever.

The plane lifts off the ground and Lillian is buckled in next to me on the sofa. It's just us with the pilot shut in the cockpit. She got up and showered again this morning. She's makeup free and her hair, which is usually smooth and sleek down her back, is now wavy and still a little damp. Her fingers are in constant motion, picking at the material of her loose dress that hits her ankles, and the new sandals I bought her are slapping against her twitching foot.

"Hey." I put a hand on her chin to tilt her face up to mine. She called to check on her grandmother this morning and whoever she talked to said there was no change overnight. "The flight is less than five hours. Try to relax."

Her beautiful brown eyes are hesitant as she searches my face ... for what, I wish I knew. "I know. Gran's house manager said she was resting comfortably now that hospice has taken over her care. I thought I'd wake up this morning in knots but knowing she's not in pain right now is comforting. She's fought cancer for over a year and is in her mid-seventies. That's not easy."

"I'm sorry, Lillian. I wish there was more I could

do. When we get back, you take as much time as you need. I'll make sure your accounts are taken care of."

I'd say I wished we weren't ambushed, weren't taken hostage, didn't have to survive in the jungle for days, but I'm a selfish bastard. I'm happy we made it out unscathed—besides the blisters on her feet—but I'd do it all over again for the fucking wake-up call. I own the damn company and don't give a shit what anyone says. Lillian Burkette isn't a fling. This is happening and I'm not worried about anything biting me in the ass. That's how sure I am about us.

She pulls her face out of my hand and looks back at her fingers, pinching her dress into a mess of wrinkles. Without looking at me, her voice is small when she says, "About work..."

The plane has leveled out, so I unbuckle and turn toward her. "What about it?"

She pulls in a big breath and, when she looks up, her face is masked with dread. "I don't know what happened between us. One minute you hated me—the next you were blowing on my blisters and being sweet. Extenuating circumstances make people do weird things. I just don't want what's happened in the last few days to affect my job. I'm prepared to forget this ever happened and go back to politely ignoring one another. I don't report directly to you so it won't be a problem. I can pretend that nothing happened so there's no need to worry."

This must be what it feels like to have your heart torn in two. It goes to show I was right. It's taken me thirty-five years ... and sure, there's an age difference. But if this is what heartbreak feels like, then I have no fucking desire to experience it, because right now, she's got me by the balls. She's so close to ruining me—she has no idea.

"Lillian." My voice is thick even though I'm doing my best to control it. I unlatch her seatbelt and flip it to the side, pulling her close to me. Her eyes go big and she finally quits worrying her dress because she's too busy worrying about my reaction. I wanted to get this out of the way last night but she was devastated by the news of her grandmother. It wasn't the right time. "If you ignore me and pretend like our time in Nicaragua didn't happen, I'll be pissed. It did happen and it's fucking real."

Her hands come to my shirt to hang on. "But you've never liked me. For months, you made that clear. You give everyone at your company the time of day except me. I'm not blind, Gabe."

"That's because I was doing my best to control myself, be the kind of CEO his employees can trust without worrying that he'll hit on them. I had to force myself to stay away from you. Had I gotten close, this would have happened. I was trying to do the right thing because the more I watched you and learned about you, I knew if you directed any of your goodness my way, I'd be screwed. And I was right."

Throughout my diatribe, her face morphs into something between awe and unbelieving bewilderment.

I close some of the distance between us. "I did my best not to cross the line with you, Lillian. I really did. I've never crossed the line—never even thought about it or wanted to with anyone at work. With you, the only way for me to fight it was to have no contact. I had to force myself to be an asshole to keep you at bay. But after this week, I don't give a shit anymore if you're my employee."

Her eyes fall to my jaw, my chest, my arms, searching for answers that are right in front of her. I'm forced to give her a squeeze to get her attention.

"You're serious?" she whispers.

I pull her into my lap, holding her close. "I'm fucking serious. And since I'm a serious person to begin with, that means something."

"I don't know what to say," she admits. "I thought you hated me."

"You don't have to say anything. Just know, I want this more than I've wanted anything and I'll prove it to you."

I can't wait another second. I dip my hand into the back of her lush hair and bring her mouth to mine.

She doesn't argue or pull away. Instead, she presses her tits into my chest and if she could crawl inside me, I think she would. Pulling my hair with a carnal tug, she holds herself to me. I might've stopped myself last night, but now, there's no way.

I let my hands explore. *Really* explore.

Dragging my touch up her side, I slide my hand between us to cup her tit. Her nipple is hard and erect under the thin fabric and, fuck me, she's not wearing a bra. She's firm, yet soft, and more than perfect, filling my hand.

All the control I've maintained around Lillian Burkette disintegrates in an instant.

I'll do everything I can to demonstrate I'm worthy and, despite the way we started, this can be good. Because, for the first time in my life, the desire to prove myself is so overwhelming, I can't control it.

"I'll make you see what I know. Swear it. I'll do anything for you," I murmur between kisses.

She moans into my mouth and my blood rushes to my dick. She makes my head spin with desire and pure fucking determination to make her mine. I move my hand up to her shoulder. Her skin is soft and fair compared to mine—dark, calloused, and scarred. It makes me feel like an animal claiming its prey, but I don't care because Lillian is gazing at me in a whole new way. I see it in her eyes.

If she's my prey, then she's running straight into the lion's den.

I finger the strap on her dress that's loose and precariously holding on. "You're bare under this."

I hardly recognize my own voice—it's something between pained and needy.

She's breathing hard, her tits rising and falling as her greedy lungs search for air. She brings her hand up to my jaw, running her fingers over my face. Her touch is a gift of permission.

It's all I need.

Sliding the strap from her shoulder, her dress falls, exposing one perfect tit. I touch her, feeling her skin-to-skin for the first time. She's pert but soft and not too big or small. For fear of sounding like a children's nursery rhyme, if Lillian Burkette didn't snore, she'd be damn near perfect.

I realize I'm toying with her pebbled nipple and

staring at her half-naked chest like a virginal teenage boy—which I abso-fucking-lutely am not. I gaze up into her milk chocolate eyes to find them heavy and mirroring the desire I feel in my cock.

Her nipple is begging to be pinched. I'm thrilled to watch her eyes close and her head fall back. Soaring at thirty-thousand feet with only a door between us and the pilot, I don't give a shit. Pressing into the center of her back, I bring her perfect tit to my mouth and suck.

She squirms in my lap, rubbing her thighs together, and, when I add my teeth, scraping her delicate skin, she presses her chest into my face for more.

Her small frame is easy to hold with one arm so I use my free hand to feel up her bare leg under her dress. Her skin is warm and smooth and when I reach to find her ass bare, I let go of her nipple with a pop.

I give her ass a squeeze and she opens her eyes. Her sweet, beautiful face is flushed, I'm not sure from which—embarrassment or desire.

"Please tell me you always go commando."

She shakes her head and licks her lips. "Only in Nicaragua."

Without taking my eyes off hers, I pull my hand over her naked hip. She doesn't look away but her breathing shallows and I slow my touch, dragging a light finger down to her pussy.

"You're smooth."

She bites her lip.

I drag my hand lower and easily slide a finger between her lips that feel no less beautiful than the ones on her face. I can't wait to kiss them.

"And wet," I add.

Her eyes fall shut and she chokes back a moan.

"Lillian," I call for her.

She has to swallow hard but she opens her eyes.

"I want you to look at me when I touch you for the first time."

She blinks slowly before focusing on me.

"Spread your legs, baby."

Wanton and ready, she does as I ask without hesitation. Her need is evident, her fingernails biting into my neck. I give myself a moment to soak this in, memorize it. Looking down at her spread across my lap, half-exposed, with shallow-breaths, and my hand up her dress, I'll never forget the first time Lillian Burkette falls apart at my touch.

"Gabe." She squirms in my lap and I look back up to her face.

"This is happening," I inform her and I start to explore her pussy, getting to know her. "I don't care what it took to get us here. I want your sweet nature in my life. I not only want your brownies and cakes, but I fucking want you to bake them in my house. And Lillian," I pause as she exhales in a huff when I pinch her clit and has to work to keep her eyes open when I slide a finger into her for the first time, "I'm a greedy bastard. I want your sweet smiles directed at me in a way that we both know I've claimed you."

She whimpers, not able to keep her eyes open any longer. The way I treated her up until a few days ago, it's a miracle I'm here right now. A miracle I don't plan to take for granted and will do everything in my power to keep.

Forever is a sappy fucking word used in the romance novels my sisters would whisper about. But right here, right now with Lillian, it's the only word circling in my mind.

If I could put this plane on auto and throw the pilot out the door, I'd strip off her dress, but that probably isn't the best idea.

Something to look forward to.

She starts to move her hips against my hand, so I give her a second finger, loving how tight she is. When I put more pressure on her clit, she widens her legs, offering me everything. She buries her face in my neck as her body begins to tense.

"Gabe," she moans and it's the sweetest sound I've ever heard.

"You're so fucking beautiful. I don't deserve you but I'm going to take you anyway."

With that, she falls apart in my arms, coming hard. I keep at her clit, circling, taking every ounce of her orgasm. I'm greedy for it.

She presses herself to my chest, clinging to me. I wrap her up but keep my hand up her dress, alternating between drawing circles on her bare ass and lower back. She doesn't move but lets her breathing even as we sit here with only the hum of the Cessna surrounding us.

She starts to push away, but I hold her close. "Don't. This is just you and me. We've got a long flight and you're gonna have one helluva day when we get you home. Let me hold you."

And that's how we sat for most of the flight.

Lillian curled in my lap, her bare tit pressed up against my chest, with my hand up her dress.

Little did I know, keeping Lillian Burkette safe in Nicaragua would be a breeze compared to the shitshow that was in store for me.

14

I'LL HOLD YOUR HAND

Lillian Burkette

"Um, Gabe?"

I look over at him as he drives me to my childhood home. He's downright gorgeous. He hasn't shaved since the day we were ambushed on that remote road in Nicaragua. I'm well acquainted with his whiskers at this point and so is my left breast. Our time in the private jet was beyond ... well, hot.

Amazing.

Out of this world.

But then after?

I'm pretty sure only Gabriel Blackburn could hold me in his lap with my top half-off and his hand up my dress while I'm wearing no panties and it be so sweet, I'd never want it to end.

I could have sat there forever. And, I did, for most of the flight.

He throws me a glance and sexy smirk that reminds me of every moment on the plane. "What, baby?"

"Turn left up here," I rattle off, my heart starting to speed. "I, well, should've taken the time on the flight to explain some things."

He reaches over and takes my hand as he steers our rental around the corner with the other. "I wouldn't change our time on the plane for anything. Tell me now."

I let him hold my hand and squeeze him tight. "My family ... they have some issues."

He doesn't look at me when he mutters, "Just wait until I tell you about my Great Aunt Libby."

"Who?"

He shakes his head. "Never mind. Tell me how odd your family is to make me feel better about mine."

"I'm not sure if odd is the right word." I take a deep breath. Vindictive and selfish come to mind. Think *Mean Girls* but switch it up with middle-aged adults who play in high society circles. "Take the next right. I told you how much my Gran means to me. How wonderful she is and how I grew up in her house, right?"

"You told me all this."

I turn to look out my window. "My parents ... they're not so wonderful. Last drive on the left. We're almost there."

"We're here to see your grandmother and she's being treated by hospice. How bad can they be?" He gives my hand a squeeze as my grandmother's estate comes into view. "Shit, Lillian. You didn't tell me you grew up on a plantation."

I exhale, worried about my Gran, nervous about my mother, and still feel a little off without panties. Gabe drives up the long drive framed by century-old trees. When he pulls around the circle and comes to a stop at the front door of the three-story southern plantation that's been in my grandfather's family for generations, I turn to him. "Please, just drop me off. You can drive right back to the airport and catch a flight to Indy. You can be home and at work by tomorrow. Just think," I try to sweeten the deal, "you can even sleep in your own bed."

He throws the SUV into park and turns to me. "I plan on sleeping in your bed. I've decided your snoring is cute as opposed to annoying and my hand has become fond of your naked ass. I can't leave you while you're naked under that dress. My hand would slap myself for the breach of my manhood. By the way, do you have extra clothes here?"

"Yes."

He raises a brow. "Panties?"

I try not to smirk. "Yes."

He gives my hand a squeeze and shakes his head. "Damn."

At any other time or place, that would make me smile, but not today and not here. "Gabe. Please. I don't want to put you through this."

He leans into me and puts the same hand that loves my rear so much on my cheek and dips into my hair. His blue eyes soften on me when he asks, "If your parents are the asswipes you've let on, who's going to hold your hand when you see your grandmother?"

I have to close my eyes so I don't start crying.

"Lillian." He gives my hair a little pull and I open my eyes to look at him. "*I'll* be the one holding your hand."

I don't answer.

"Okay," he answers for me and then leans in to press his lips to mine. "Let's do this."

Oh, my. He has no idea.

―――――

Gabriel Blackburn

"What is that horrendous thing you're wearing?"

"You were supposed to be here yesterday and now you show up unannounced and looking like that? We could have had guests."

"Did you glance in a mirror before you decided it would be a good idea to waltz out your door ... in *that*?"

"Oh my God, Lillian. If your hair isn't bad enough, you're covered in bug bites. Why would you subject yourself to that? You're going to get the Zika virus."

"Who is *he* and why did you bring a stranger here? He's wearing *shorts*."

Well, fuck me.

I only want to know one thing—how did these douchewads produce my sweet Lillian?

Her father, the one who apparently doesn't wear

shorts, is fully gray and would be glaring down his nose at me through his beady little glasses if he didn't have to look up to meet my gaze. I'm not even sure he's looking through the glasses. My guess is they're an odd accessory.

And her mother, the germaphobe, is taller than her husband and sports a short, bleached-blond do. She must be a football fan since her hair is shaped sort of dome-like and resembles a helmet the size of an NFL linebacker's.

Meanwhile, Lillian is standing next to me, speechless and pantyless. The latter, I cannot stop thinking about.

She glances up at me and, while I feel like I've experienced a great deal of her expressions over the past week, this one is nothing but pure dread mixed with embarrassment. She knew this would happen and didn't want me to experience it.

She winces before turning to Mr. and Mrs. Doom and Gloom, stepping forward like a robot fresh out of the Stick Up Your Ass Finishing School. "Mother, Daddy, I'd like to introduce Gabriel Blackburn. He's my—"

"Boyfriend," I interrupt, stepping forward and wrapping my arm around Lillian to stake my claim. I try not to wince as the word tumbles out of my mouth. I'm thirty-five. Do thirty-five-year-olds refer to themselves as a *boyfriend*? I sure as hell never thought I would. "Man. Courter. Whatever you want to call me, I'm not picky. I'm *with* Lillian."

"Ooooh, my," Lillian whispers from my side.

"Lillian!" Mrs. Helmet Head exclaims. "Tell me this isn't so."

Her father intensifies his glare and, if the sun were out, he might be able to start a fire with those damn glasses. "I'd like to speak with my daughter alone, young man."

Again, I'm thirty-fucking-five. There's no *young man* in the room.

I shake my head. "You both must be blind because Lillian looks beautiful, especially after having a rough few days. We had some issues while traveling and lost our luggage. Now, if you'll excuse us, Lillian wants to see her grandmother." I look down at Lillian who's standing like a statue, her front pressed to my side. Her eyes are wide and she looks like she might faint. "Where's your Gran, baby?"

"Baby?" Lillian's big-headed mother actually *tsks* me. If we don't get out of here soon, I might lose my shit on these *Gone with the Wind* uppity assholes.

I give Lillian another squeeze.

She winces. "The library."

"Right. Let's go."

"Wait just one second," Mr. Beady Eyes tries again.

"Lillian!" her mother calls after us.

Lillian stops and turns back to the people who, from the looks of it, gave her life but that's about it. "I don't want to see you and I don't want to talk to you. I'm going to sit with Gran until she leaves this earth ... while all you're doing is waiting for this to be yours," she flips her hand in a circle, "not caring about her one bit. Don't show your face in the library and ruin my last moments with the woman I love more than anything."

My sweet Lillian. She snores, she can traipse through a jungle, be brave when taken hostage, melt in my arms, and still show her backbone to her asshole parents.

And I can't wait to taste her brownies among other sweet things she has to offer.

I'm never letting her go.

15

YOU COULD BREAK ME

Lillian Burkette

I LIVED HERE my entire life until I left for college. The mansion is big enough for five more families, so it never seemed like a big deal to me for us to live with my grandmother. When I was old enough to see my parents for what they were, it was easy to see why they'd prefer living here rather than making their own way. They never had to lift a finger.

My father works for my mother's family business. My grandfather founded it when he was young. His family might come from big money, but he used that and made it bigger.

My mother, on the other hand, lunches and gossips.

But not Gran. She grew up with little before she met my Gramps and never forgot where she came from. She taught me to bake, make sausage gravy to the perfect consistency, and to tend a garden. When I got older, she explained how she made mistakes with my mother and took full responsibility of raising an entitled child who grew into a selfish adult. I always told her she was too hard on herself. My mother is who she is.

Gran said I was her second chance, that the day I was born she promised herself she'd do everything in her power to make sure I didn't end up like my mother. I was the only reason she allowed my parents to live on the plantation because, in her words, living with my parents was a *cocklebur in her soft, southern tush*.

I sat with her all day and Gabe made good on his promise. He not only held my hand but wrapped me up in his arms as we sat here and took in her unconscious, lifeless body as it wilted away from me. Besides the hospice nurse, no one else has stepped foot in the library besides the house manager who brought dinner to us.

Gabe left me for about an hour and a half, telling me he had to run some errands, promising he'd be back. He returned with coffee and a slew of chocolate treats that I barely picked at.

I just can't.

"You should get some rest, Miss Lillian," the night nurse whispers. "Don't you worry your pretty head. I'll send for you straight away if there's any change. I promise, she's not in any pain."

I hear Gabe, who was sitting in a wingback chair next to my Gramps' antique desk, move in behind me. He puts his hand to my chin and lifts my face. "She's right. You should sleep."

The mention of sleep makes me realize how stiff I am from sitting in this chair most of the day listening to my sweet Gran's shallow, tortured breaths. I've seen a lot of death in the past week, but watching cancer slowly eat away at the woman I adore is an evil pain deep in my heart.

I lean up and press a kiss to Gran's wrinkled forehead. What's left of her once thick and lush gray hair is lying limp, swept away from her equally gray, clammy face. I choke back a sob and the next thing I know, I'm up in Gabe's arms.

He carries me down the hall and when we head up the grand staircase I used to play on as a child, I realize he's heading straight to my old room.

When he sits on the bed with me in his lap, I notice all the bags sitting around. Bags from the Apple store, department stores, Target, and even Banana Republic.

"Where did all that come from?" I sniff and wipe my face on his shirt, realizing I've done this way too much this week. "And how did they get in here?"

"It turns out the house manager likes me more than your parents do. He was more than happy to tell me where your room is. I got us both new MacBooks and phones. It might feel like I'm in a movie from the 1800's on your plantation, but we still need to communicate with the outside world. And I needed some clothes and a toothbrush. The Welcoming Committee didn't like my shorts."

"It's not my plantation," I argue. "And I like you in shorts."

He leans in to kiss me. "And I like you pantyless.

I'm going to take a shower. It's been a long day. You should get some sleep."

I nod and climb out of his arms even though I don't want to. Gabe presses his lips to the top of my head and grabs three Target bags and disappears into my childhood bathroom that is still wallpapered with buttercups the color of a bright, sunny day.

I go to my pine dresser and pull out a pair of panties and a nightgown from college as I listen to my shower turn on. Looking at myself in the mirror hanging over my dresser, I shut the drawer with my hip and really take in my reflection for the first time since we were ambushed.

I look different.

I never let my hair air dry. I never go without makeup. And I absolutely never go without a bra and panties. My eyes fall to my loose dress hanging on my breasts and my nipples that are beading through the rayon fabric.

Dragging my hands up my body, over my breasts and skin covered in bug bites and scrapes, I take in the woman I see in the mirror. I stood up to my parents for the first time today. I'm the adult now to my dying Gran who was always the one to take care of me. She showed me who I want to be and made me who I am.

It doesn't matter what people think—if Gran taught me anything, it was that.

Pushing away from the dresser, I turn and make long strides to my bathroom. Turning the antique crystal doorknob, I pad barefoot over the beehive tile laid in black and white, past the clawfoot tub sitting under the leaded glass window and come to a stop in front of the modern shower that was updated in the last decade.

Gabe is standing with his side to me, one hand leaning on the carrera wall with his head under the stream of water. Steam surrounds him, creating a dreamy-like frame for his perfect body. Sculpted of nothing but muscle, his wide shoulders and chest narrow as my eyes drop over his perfectly rounded behind and thick thighs. My heart speeds and I can't take my eyes off his cock—seeing him for the first time. It's perfect, thick and long, even relaxed as he stands in my shower, soaking up the hot water.

When I reach for the handle and open the door, he jerks and turns to me. Now, with nothing between us, him standing in front of me stark naked, he makes no move. He doesn't even give me a hint of what he's thinking.

I allow myself one more look, never wanting to forget a moment of today. A day where Gabriel Blackburn made sure I got home where I need to be and has done nothing but care for me.

"Lillian."

His voice, the first hint that I might have the same effect on him as he does me, is gravelly and deep.

When his cock twitches, my eyes fly back to his.

My fingers don't waste any more time. I lift my hands to the spaghetti straps of my dress, pulling them down my shoulders with such ease I'm surprised they hung on all day. Gravity takes over and as soon as my dress hits the bathmat, Gabe's big, wet hand grabs mine.

There're no questions.

There's no talking.

There's nothing more that needs to be said.

Right now, I need to lose myself in him.

Gabe turns me and presses my back against the shower wall, the water falling around us like one body instead of two. His cock, now even longer and impossibly thick, is standing at attention and pressed into my tummy. My breasts are rising and falling. His hands move on my arms, my sides, my hips.

The next thing I know, he picks me up and my legs are wrapped around his waist and the tip of his cock teases my sex.

To get lost in Gabe. I want it more than anything.

I need it.

He doesn't move, but his steel eyes are darker and more intense than I've ever seen.

It's up to me. He hasn't said a word, but somehow, I just know.

I want him to make me forget about losing my Gran, dealing with my parents, and everything that happened in Nicaragua. But more than anything, I want him.

Without taking my eyes off his, I sink down onto his cock, slowly, feeling the delicious ache of him stretching me. When he fills me completely, his lids fall and an expression sweeps over his face that's nothing but pure ecstasy.

I wrap one hand around his neck and the other up the back of his head to hold on, because I might have been the one to instigate this, but when Gabe opens his eyes, I know he'll be the one to take over.

And he does.

Using what feels like every muscle in his body, he slams into me the rest of the way. Just when I didn't think I could take more of him, Gabe takes all of me. Filling me to the root, he takes a step back and sits on my shower bench, bringing me down on his lap, still connected. He drags his hand down the center of my body, his eyes following his path. Looking down his chest to where we're connected, he spreads me and finds my clit. When his thumb moves, so do I, rocking on his shaft, loving the way he fills me and makes my body hum.

Hanging on to his strong shoulders, my head starts to fall back when he calls for me.

"No. Don't look away. Watch what I'm doing to you, baby."

Oh, my.

"You're so fucking sweet. Everything about you. I'm a lucky man."

I bite my lip and do my best to keep my eyes open because I feel it. I'm so close to the edge.

"Watch me work your clit, baby."

I look down my naked body to where we're connected. His scarred hand between us, dark and calloused on my fair skin, is the perfect representation of us. We're different but that's what makes it so good.

"I want you to come before I fuck you for the first time. Because, baby, the second you sank your sweet little pussy down on my cock, you gave me you. I'm not letting go."

I can't answer him. Watching him work my clit

and listening to him is too much. No one's ever talked to me this way before. Sex has never been raw and carnal and so, so heady.

I rock faster, my nails biting into the skin on his neck and shoulders. I feel it and it's going to be like nothing I've experienced.

When it starts to come over me, I lose Gabe's thumb. His hand comes to my ass to help me move. "There you go. Fuck yourself and find it, sweet Lillian. Show me you can."

I'm so close. I rock harder, doing everything I can to find contact where I need it most. I think of nothing but the ache that needs tending between my legs.

"So fucking beautiful. I wish you could see yourself."

Not caring who's under the same roof as us, I call out, holding myself to him, pressing down on his cock where I pulse.

"You're damned perfect," Gabe rumbles in my ear and the next thing I know, my back is to the wall and he's fucking me.

His hand comes up to cup the back my head against the tile. He's using such strength and power, he drags out my orgasm and I whimper into the side of his face.

His back muscles tense where I'm holding on and he brutally slams into me two more times before planting himself so deep, I'm sure to feel where he's been for a week.

And I hope I do.

Right now, I hope I never lose this feeling.

"I'm a strong man, but you could break me, Lillian. Only you could bring a man like me to my knees."

I put my lips to his neck where my face is pressed and where I never want to leave. "I'd never break you, Gabe. Never."

"But you could," he murmurs in my ear and presses his cock into me one more time. Fisting my hair, he holds me steady and looks straight into my eyes. "And that makes you the most powerful woman in my world."

16

BY MY SIDE

Lillian Burkette

My Gran died late the next day.

Gabe was by my side.

Gabe handled my parents.

Gabe handled everything.

But most of all, he loved me. He didn't say it, but he showed it.

Which made him the most powerful person in *my* world.

17

YOU'RE FIRED
THREE WEEKS LATER...

Lillian Burkette

It's been about a month since I've been to the office.

One week in Central America and three weeks in North Carolina.

Gabe stayed with me through Gran's funeral. He stayed with me during the reading of her last will and testament, stating that her estate—and everything in it—was to skip a generation. Everything was bequeathed to me.

Me.

There was a clause stating that my parents were to be given the right to live in the small guest house on the property until they could make other arrangements. It wasn't like my parents were left with nothing. My mother still had her trust and my father a good job with the family business in which I now held a majority of the shares.

Suffice it to say, my parents started World War III.

Gabe stayed through that, too.

But after working out of my childhood bedroom every day, he finally had to head back to Indy for a product rollout. That was a week and a half ago. I had to stay to make sure everything was in order before I left.

My parents are contesting the will, but, by court order, have moved out of my grandmother's home until it's settled.

I don't care what happens. My grandmother loved me and I loved her. I have twenty-six years of memories. I brought back some of her things I want to keep forever. If the will isn't overturned, I'm not sure what I'll do with the plantation. The property is on the National Register. It can't be broken up or sold and I want to do everything I can to make sure it looks just like it does now for as long as I live.

If my parents aren't a part of that, so be it.

I flew back to Indy yesterday afternoon and Gabe picked me up at the airport. I wore my Nicaraguan sundress and the second he laid eyes on me, he knew. He took me straight to his house and we barely made it through the front door.

I wasn't wearing anything underneath. Just for him.

He'd barely kicked the front door shut when he ripped my dress off—literally ripping it this time. After he put his mouth between my legs and sucked on my clit until I came, he took me up against the wall. I was completely naked and he was completely clothed.

It was all Gabe and I loved it.

Then he drove me back to my apartment and made me pack a big bag and said for the time being, he wanted me in his bed. He actually said he missed my snoring. He didn't even smirk when he said this so I couldn't tell if he was serious or not but he was dead serious about me being in his bed.

Now, it's my first day back at work and I'm not just Lillian Burkette, Marketing Representative for the Central America Territory.

No.

I'm Lillian Burkette, the woman who's sleeping with her boss's boss.

I've dreaded this day for weeks. I've worried about it out loud to Gabe, who brushes it off. Sure, it's easy for him. He owns the company.

I've gotten plenty of emails and phone calls over the last few weeks, checking on me and offering their condolences. I've even had a couple co-workers ask why the CEO stayed with me in North Carolina at all, let alone as long as he did. I brushed them off, using my Gran's death as an excuse. Of course, they want to know and Gabe didn't do much to keep it on the downlow. It was easy for everyone to see—humans are curious creatures by nature.

The writing was on the wall and it might as well have been graffitied in enormous, red letters—I was sleeping with the boss's boss. News like that doesn't sit quietly. It spreads like wildfire.

Assuming everyone has figured out Gabe and I are together, I rushed through my co-workers this morning who all offered me sweet hellos and condolences on the way in. But knowing that they know, I'm not sure I can do this. It makes me literally ill wondering what they're thinking of me.

I've only been here for thirty minutes, I have an ache in my stomach, and am afraid to leave my office. Gabe came to work an hour before me this morning for a meeting, so I haven't seen him yet.

With nervous, sweaty hands, I pick up my cell to bring up his text string.

Me – People have to know about us by now.

Gabe – Then let them know. I have nothing to hide.

Me – Of course, you don't. You own the company. They're probably whispering about me. I'm the one who's doing naughty things with the CEO.

I see bubbles, then they disappear. Bubbles. No bubbles.

Gabe – Baby, it's eight-thirty in the morning on your first day back and you're making me hard. How am I supposed to make it 'til lunch with you sexting me like this?

I gasp.

Me – We are not having lunch sex!

Gabe – With all this talk of sex, we're definitely hitting it at lunch.

Me – Gabe, stop it.

Me – Just stop.

Gabe – You won't be asking me to stop at lunch.

My computer dings.

I look up and I have a meeting request from Gabriel Blackburn from noon to one.

The nerve!

I reject the meeting.

Me – Gabe, I'm serious. I don't know if I can take this.

Gabe – Fine. You're fired.

My eyes go big and I stare at my phone.

What? He fired me?

Oh, no. He did *not* just fire me.

Putting my phone down, I march out of my small office. Walking through the cubicles and outlying areas, I make my way to a space I've never entered before. The office of the owner-slash-CEO-slash-my lover.

I nod quickly to the marketing director, my manager, looking away just as fast, while ignoring everyone else. When I get to the swanky corner space, I pass by Gabe's assistant and don't knock or warn him I'm coming in.

I shut the door behind me. It feels like we're in a fishbowl in his glass-walled office. I glance over my shoulder to find I'm right but a fishbowl doesn't do it justice.

We might as well be in an aquarium at the zoo.

I turn back to Gabe who's sitting behind his desk. He has the nerve to smirk. "I knew you wouldn't be able to stay away 'til lunch."

I ignore him. "You fired me? Seriously?"

At least he doesn't get up and come to me. Since we've been together, it's rare we're in the same room with this much distance between us. "You said you didn't know if you could take this," he points his finger up in the air and circles it, "and since this," he motions between the two of us, "is happening, I thought I'd help you out."

"I'm not letting you fire me," I declare. I know it's stupid but I don't know what else to say.

"Well, I'm certainly not allowing you to change the status of us, so either you get over what everyone might be thinking or I'll help you find another job. It won't be hard. You're good at what you do. I'd hate to lose you here, but, baby, I won't allow you to leave me. If I have to start a new company for you to work at, I will."

I exhale, feeling defeated and, if I'm honest, just a little bit turned on by how much he wants *us* to happen. "I just don't want to be *that woman*, because I'm not. I work hard and earn my way, not sleep with my boss for any type of favors."

He frowns and gets up to move. Lucky for me, he still doesn't come to me. He crosses his arms and perches his beautiful backside on the front of his desk. "You'd better not be sleeping with your boss. I'm going to have an issue with that."

I tip my head. "You know what I mean."

He gives me a small smile. "Baby, come here."

I widen my eyes. "No. You have to promise not to do that here at work. Please, Gabe."

He sighs and looks out his glass-walled office. He seems to make a decision and pushes away from the desk. I have to take a step back, almost tripping on my spiked heel, but he moves around me at a quick clip and opens his office door.

Standing outside his office, he raises his voice to a

point that it booms through the vast space. "I need your attention."

"Oh, no," I whisper to myself in horror.

"There will be days when I give Lillian Burkette a ride to work. There might be other days when I give her a ride home. Some days, like today, I'll also take her to lunch. Raise your hand if you have an issue with this."

All my co-workers are either looking over cubicles or standing in the doorways to their offices. A murmur spreads through the space as every single person shakes their head or shrugs with "no's" and "no way, boss," and "no problem here."

"Very good." Gabe nods and stuffs his hands in his pockets. "I don't want to hear anything about it. Get back to work."

The regular office hustle and bustle returns to its normal level and Gabe returns to me but doesn't shut the door. He leaves at least two feet between us and lowers his voice for only my ears. "I really want to kiss you right now."

I close my eyes in defeat. I know he won't but I love how he always puts it out there. With Gabe, I never wonder what he's thinking.

"And I'm going to fuck you at lunch. Be ready to go by noon. I've got a meeting at one-thirty, we'll have to be fast so I can still swing by and pick you up a sandwich and a brownie."

I open my eyes and his gaze is hot and heavy. He looks like he'd eat me up right now if I were to give him the green light.

"Morning sex," he goes on. "That might be the only way I can get through a day working with you."

I smile. "No more announcements. Please?"

"Don't worry, baby. It'll work out and you'll be fine. You got through the last month. Sleeping with the big boss is a piece of cake."

Well, that's the truth. "Okay."

We part ways, him to his desk and me, making my walk of shame back to my office. But this time I did it caring less because I'm really looking forward to lunch.

EPILOGUE
SIX MONTHS LATER...

Gabriel Blackburn

STANDING IN THE gardens of Lillian's plantation under the heavy moss-covered limbs of almost three-hundred-year-old live oaks, I look over at my wife of about two hours. She's talking to Melody Keegan and Maya Cain while holding a glass of champagne.

I swear, the woman is capable of feeling my eyes on her no matter where we are because she glances my direction and smooths her hand down her flat stomach over the silk of her gown. Giving me a small smile, she raises her glass to me but doesn't take a sip.

No one knows. She doesn't want to tell anyone for a couple months.

Hell, she only told me last week.

"Congratulations." I turn to see my buddy from Ranger school, Grady Cain.

I take his outstretched hand and shake it. "Thanks, man."

"No," he smirks at me, "I mean *congratulations*. On the baby."

I frown. "How did you know?"

He tips his head to the three women talking. "Your new wife has been holding that glass for over an hour and hasn't taken a sip. It's hot as fuck out here—no way would anyone still want to drink that shit after losing its chill. You might want to tell her to grab a new glass if you don't want anyone to know."

I shake my head.

Grady Cain was discharged from the Army and fell off the face of the earth a year after we graduated Ranger school. Word is he's been doing some top-secret shit, but he's never offered, so I never asked. He surfaced a few years ago and is back in the States, settled down with a wife, kid, and with another on the way.

"Don't mention it to anyone," I warn. "No one at work knows and we're not ready for the questions yet. Lillian has started a foundation for the plantation and it's time consuming. She's thinking it could be a full-time gig if she opens it to the public and donates the proceeds back to the community."

Lillian's parents were denied every motion they filed to contest her grandmother's will. Two months ago, the estate was settled and my wife now owns this fucker and all the land it sits on. Since we're settled in Indy, she said she wants to open it to the public. Now that her parents are out of the picture, she can move forward.

Her parents weren't invited to the wedding.

This was an easy decision and one I'm happy my sweet as hell wife didn't feel guilt over. No way did I want to see their faces on this day after the shit they put Lillian through.

"Never thought I'd see the day Gabe Blackburn would get married, let alone be a daddy."

I look over to see Crew Vega and I frown at him. "The fuck?"

"I still don't understand how you got someone as perfect as her to like you, let alone marry you." He raises his beer and watches our wives chatter. "But here's to little Blackburns running amuck. I hope they make you gray. Your hair is too perfect."

"Does everyone know about the baby?" I ask.

I know nothing about pregnancy—other than drugs and alcohol are bad. I also know nothing about babies. All I know is I'll never subject my kid to the horrors of my Great Aunt Libby's cats—dead or alive. I also know I probably won't be able to stop my mother and sisters from pushing their classic musicals on my offspring. I don't have enough power in the world to put a stop to that.

Crew looks back to me. "It's plain to see. Your woman can't keep her hand off her stomach."

Interesting. Neither can I since she told me my sperm was the strongest in all the land since it took no effort at all to get her pregnant. She did away with her pills last month after talking me into the fact small humans will make our lives better. Since my life is fan-fucking-tastic right now, I'll basically do anything she wants.

Except get a cat.

We'll never have a fucking cat.

I'll buy her a dog after the honeymoon.

Hell, I'll buy her a ferret if she wants one, but I draw the line at cats.

"Here's to settling down." Grady raises his water glass. Crew and I follow suit with our beers when Grady adds, "May you have all girls and they look just like your new wife so you will forever be surrounded by pink and be on punkass-boy patrol."

I click my glass to theirs and glare at Grady. "You're an asshole."

"We got your back, man." Grady grins. "We make people disappear."

I ignore that statement for fear of being an accessory to a crime and because I see Great Aunt Libby pull my sweet Lillian away from her new friends.

"Excuse me. I need to save my wife before my aunt ropes us into a visit."

I make my way across the lawn to the tents where dinner will be served in about an hour and the air-conditioned space where our tiered chocolate wedding cake is displayed. Lillian explained to me that humidity and icing don't mix well.

"...I'm Gabe's favorite aunt. He just loved to visit me when he was little."

I wrap a hand around Lillian's waist and pull her back to my front. Splaying my hand over our miniature human, I greet the crazy cat lady. "Hi, Libby. Thanks for coming."

"Well, I was just talking to your bride here about

when you were little. I can't wait to get to know her. I do hope you'll come for a visit soon."

"We'd love to have you at our house. Lillian will bake you a cake. Right, baby?" I look down at my wife and give her a squeeze.

When she smiles up at me, she's so damn beautiful, I realize Crew is right. It's nothing short of a miracle she gave me the time of day, let alone agreed to marry me. Even now, with the small human on the way, it's hard to believe she's mine.

"Of course." Lillian grins at me. I was forced to spill one night before the wedding about my cat phobia so she'd have my back in case something like this happened. Like the kickass wife she's proven to be over the last two hours, she turns her southern charm on my aunt. "You have to come to our house. Nothing would make me happier than to create new memories with Gabe's family as we start our lives together. I'll cook and bake for you and you can stay as long as you like."

I frown. Now she's just going overboard.

"If you'll excuse us, Libby, I'd like a moment with my bride."

"I'll call you," Aunt Libby yells after us as I drag Lillian away. "You have to answer because I don't text."

Lillian waves at her as I pull her into the gardening shed that's really just a fancy building for flowers.

"Aunt Libby is sweet," Lillian says as I close her in and put her back to the wall.

"She's not. Don't let her fool you. She's a freak." I

take her in my arms and put my lips to her skin where her neck meets her shoulder.

"Don't worry, Gabe. I'll protect you from the cats."

I lift my head and frown. "That's not funny."

Her smile grows big. "I know. Cats are no joke."

I bring my hands to her face and change the subject. "You married me."

Her face softens. "I did."

"You won't regret it."

She shakes her head in my hands. "Never."

"Love you, baby."

"Gabe." My whispered name floats across my face and, like every time she does it, it's a fucking gift I'll never take for granted since I wouldn't be here right now if it had been left up to my own damn stubbornness. "I love you, too."

And for the millionth time, I thank God we were ambushed in a Nicaraguan rainforest.

Four years later...

"Why?"

I fill my travel mug with coffee and look over at my wife who's exhausted and run down. I know this because I feel the same fucking way, I just don't look it because I've at least had a shower to wake my ass up. She's in a sweatshirt that I'm pretty sure she's worn three days in a row with spit-up, breast milk, and coffee stains on the front. Imma, who was named after Lillian's Gran, is sitting at her feet in our kitchen and has just dragged all the tupperware out of the cabinets, pretending to cook. Rosco, our four-year-old black lab who still acts like a puppy, is right next to Imma, chewing the fuck out of a plastic lid and all I can think of is I'm going to find that in his dog shit the next time I mow.

Lillian keeps on. "I don't understand why she won't sleep more than thirty minutes at a time at night and look at her now? She's sleeping like a baby, like she should be, because she is one."

I set down my coffee and reach for my youngest daughter. Izzy, who's just as perfect as her older sister, is snoozing away in her swing. She's four months old and, since I'm a baby expert, I know she should be sleeping at least four to five hours at a time, if not longer.

On my wedding day, Grady Cain put a curse on me and it stuck. So far, I'm outnumbered in this house, three to one, if I don't count the dog. All girls so far, but in about nine months, I'll start sweet talking my wife into small human number three. It only took me a day to convince her to let my sperm do what it does best before I knocked her up with number two, so this means the sooner I can get Izzy to sleep through the night, the sooner I can let my boys free again.

Izzy stretches in my hands as I hold her up to my face. "Izzy, we need to conference about something important." Her fists rub her eyes and she yawns, drawing her chubby little legs up. She's just as bone-tired as the rest of us. "Your mommy is gonna keep you awake as much as possible today. You're not going to go in the car, or listen to the hair dryer, or hang out by the laundry room. There will be no white noise for you all day. And tonight, you're going to sleep in your own room for the first time—"

"No!" Lillian argues. "She's too little. We need to keep her close where we can hear her."

I ignore my wife. "—in a room that your father spent a fuckin' mint to decorate—"

"Gabe! Watch your language."

"—not to mention all the high-tech equipment I've installed to watch you from everywhere in the house *and* our phones *and* our computers because your father not only has the strongest sperm around—"

"Would you quit with the sperm?"

"—but he's also a technological genius." I smile at my daughter who's now sort of awake and reaching for my nose. "And you know what, baby? You're gonna sleep so good tonight because your mommy won't wake you up with her snoring."

"Gabe Blackburn. I do not wake her up."

I look down at my tired but beautiful wife. "I love you, but you do. She's sleeping with the giraffes tonight. It makes my stomach turn every time I think about how much money I spent on that damn room—it's time for some return on our investment."

Lillian's tired, brown-eyed gaze floats to our baby who I've got settled in the crook of my arm that was made just for her. "She's too little to be away from us."

I lean in to kiss my wife's forehead. "We're not sending her to boarding school. She'll be in the next room, with a well-insulated wall between us so she can get some shut-eye. Trust me. I know babies. Now, go take a long shower. I can skip my first meeting."

My sweet Lillian doesn't head for the shower, she falls into my chest. I wrap her up in my free arm and put my lips to the top of her messy-haired head that really needs to be washed. "I love you."

Imma has wrapped herself around my leg, sitting on my Magnanni Italian leather dress shoe.

"Daddy!"

I look down at my oldest human. "Yeah, baby?"

"Fuckin' mint!"

Lillian's body tenses and I tighten my hold on her so she can't move.

"Gabe!"

"Shh." I put my lips to her head, holding her in a vice grip. "That didn't happen. You're tired and hallucinating."

Rosco jumps on me, barking, and Imma giggles, pulling at my leg. "Gimme a ride, Daddy."

Lillian looks up at me and gives me a tired smile and shakes her head.

"Aren't you glad you married me?" I ask her this every time I find a way to annoy her.

She lifts up on her tired toes and puts her lips to my jaw. "Everyday. I love you."

With Imma yanking my leg, Rosco about to hump me, and Izzy grabbing at Lillian's hair, I pull my wife up to kiss her long, hard, and deep. When I let her mouth go, I tell her the truth. "You still bring me to my knees, baby. The most powerful person in the world."

Thank you for reading and I hope you enjoyed the story of Gabe and Lillian.
Read Crew Vega's book, Vines
Read Grady Cain's book, Paths
All my books are available to read for free with Kindle Unlimited.

A NOTE FROM THE AUTHOR

I HAVE SO many people to thank for their help in the final product of *Blackburn*. I needed this book turned around quickly and my team was there for me, just like always.

Elle, thank you for always pushing me when I feel stuck in the writing muck. I can't believe Gabe is a close second to Cam for you. That's huge! Kristan, you not only fit me in your tight schedule, but polished my words to make them pretty as a picture. I adore you and the team we've become. Shannon Brown, thank you for our morning sprints. Could not have finished this on time without you. Laurie, Ivy, Kolleen, Carrie, Gillian, and Gi—you're the best beta team. I don't know what I'd do without you. To Layla Frost and Sarah Curtis, your proofs and daily support mean everything.

To my Review Team—I've come to love our group. Thank you for being there for me to read all my words.

A Note from the Author

And to all my readers and bloggers—I can't say enough. Thank you for coming back for more with every book. I'll never take you for granted.

Every time I sit down to write a book, I like to find a way to challenge myself. A different type of character or a new trope. My goal was to write a workplace romance but do it differently than I've ever read. I also wanted to write an over-the-top, all-in, possessive, yet sweet, egotistical hero.

Lillian is Gabe's yin to his yang.

I hope you loved them as much as I loved writing their story.

OTHER BOOKS BY BRYNNE ASHER

The Carpino Series

Overflow – The Carpino Series, Book 1

Beautiful Life – The Carpino Series, Book 2

Athica Lane – The Carpino Series, Book 3

Until Avery – A Carpino Series Crossover Novella

Killers Series

Vines – A Killers Novel, Book 1

Paths – A Killers Novel, Book 2

Gifts – A Killers Novel, Book 3

Veils – A Killers Novel, Book 4

Scars – A Killers Novel, Book 5

Until the Tequila – A Killers Crossover Novella

The Montgomery Series

Bad Situation – The Montgomery Series, Book 1

Broken Halo – The Montgomery Series, Book 2

Standalones

Blackburn

The Dillon Sisters

Deathly by Brynne Asher

Damaged by Layla Frost

ABOUT THE AUTHOR

BRYNNE ASHER LIVES in the Midwest with her husband, three children and her perfect dog. When she isn't creating pretend people and relationships in her head, she's running her kids around and doing laundry. She enjoys decorating and shopping, always seeking the best deal. A perfect day in "Brynne World" ends in front of an outdoor fire with family, friends, s'mores, and a delicious cocktail.

Printed in Great Britain
by Amazon